Earthers were dismayed but they learned to accept the loss of Mer Folk, Fairies and Elves, keeping them alive in memory with mythical stories.

By the time early humans realized these delightful creatures existed, there were only remote groups left to move.

In Aelwen's time only a single troop of twenty-three Fairies survived.

They were the source of the life energy on Enceladus. Providing nothing happened to end their lives, these could live comfortably another 10,000 years.

The Titans and Muir-Gheilt were flourishing but of the entire Elvan race, there remained but twelve led by Sioned. He was, by his own admission, centuries old and he was the baby among them.

https://jkayshively.info/

jkshively@jkayshively.info

Dedicated to

First and foremost: The One God

then

My children Ted and Tamra
And ALL my Grandchildren
Including my first Great Grandchild

And let's not forget my Aunt Bonnie
My Sis Pat and my Niece Rose

Here's to finding the ship that hit the moon!

CHAPTER ONE

Endarra set the ship down in Kyra with barely a thump. Hers was only one of fifty-five giant spaceships, acquired in the Jukara Cloud Galaxy, known on Earth as the Large and Small Magellanic Cloud Galaxies.

Their cargo was live and the Empagosans had charged the crews with the engineering of some underwater cities and some islands in the domes naturally developed under the crust of Enceladus.

They were told earlier they didn't need to concern themselves with the other ships. The twenty or so that carried the mer-demons (Merrow of the Ancient Lands) as some of their crew called them.

Good thing they were separated by the air membrane! She chuckled as the idea of those war mongering dogs being cowed by that lot was actually very funny.

The engineers on those ships were the dregs of the free trade zones generations back. But they were great for dirty work.

For centuries their kind had served those on Titan well! Titan held minerals needed everywhere. These, called Varrain, did all the mining topside and under.

They were educated in their field and rarely mingled with the rest of the population. They knew next to nothing about society and lived in camps like the nomads they were.

She glanced at the screen showing the ships logs and noted they had just been updated by Briggia, the ship's Engineer, grinning as she saw the description of the landing as lighter than a maben.

Maben being the Muir-Gheilt offspring they were set to unload into the ocean after a long, much needed rest.

She shook her head. This was going to be the mission of her life. They promised a life change the likes of which the Universe had not seen since shortly after its creation when the Fallen swooped in from the Heavens.

The scenes from the database entries flashed through her mind. The wanton carnage, the sexual deviancies, the monsters born as they ripped through their mother's wombs.

The Nephilim, as they were called, knew no restrictions. Not bound by the One, being an abomination that existed devoid of souls. With no conscience. Not even hell would take them.

They were ravenous, and their favorite food was human.

Where the Fallen were of equal size to humans, the Nephilim were not. There was no mating with the humans though filled with every kind of lust. The result was fury.

As they were mortal, they eventually died out. However, not before decimating nearly half the human population of earth. The remaining half rebuilt society from the debris.

A little more serious Endarra entered the communal area of her ship. The trek there had been invigorating and she was beginning to need food. There was to be a victory feast as they began their new lives. But in the meantime, one needed sustenance.

It would be some time before the others arrived. Perhaps they would never arrive. However, if they did, they would be in dire need of these cities.

Endarra quietly walked into the throng focused on Balor, the Second in Command. He was giving orders to stay shipside until Sioned and his cohorts did whatever they were going to do.

As it was explained, to be in the water which held some of the properties of everything in it, was to subject one's self to wild and unfettered magic. While Sioned and crew worked to make Kyra habitable, that is.

Watching from the portholes, however, was not a problem. Everyone was rushing to stake a claim on seats by observation windows.

The Titans among them may never share what they were to witness. But the Varrain were nearly indestructible. They might live long enough to tell those in the next wave of ships. The oldest included in this trip were nearly 4000 years old and considered middle aged. Their pregnancies lasted 100 years for female Varrain.

"Hey there!" The luscious brunette called out to the throng as Balor took a breath. "We have time to rest and eat before it begins." The group that had already headed for the seats were really going to miss out.

Endarra's violet eyes scanned the crowd, looking for Braghdoen, Doon for short. He hadn't arrived yet. She would eat and wait.

The leader of the *dogs* was her latest fling. *She never thought they were undesirable after all. She just made good and sure there was no chance she could become impregnated.* He shouldn't be long. It was going to be a really nice rest time!

"Captain?" Sioned appeared at her shoulder. "We have a problem. There is nothing we can do here until we locate Gria."

Startled, Endarra looked up at the Ancient Elf. "What do you mean? I just saw her at my early meal."

She wondered where the tiny fairy might go to hide. Perhaps she was overwhelmed by the feat they were to perform.

After all, everyone knew they would lose at least half their magic in the act of creating a place for life here. But they signed up for this, so it was expected the elves and fairies would follow through. *All* of them.

They had a sacred duty to install it in the moon's core. What *it was* was a subject that had whiled away the many long hours of the trip.

The secret would not be wheedled out of the fae folk nor the elvish. Tight lipped and merciless they kept to themselves to avoid the temptation to talk. They loved to talk. This must be beyond the ken of any outside their clans. It must be unimaginable.

She narrowed her eyes and focused on her meal, hearing the chair opposite scrape back. Not giving in to her intense desire to wrap her leg around the long legs belonging to Doon.

Grateful that she hadn't as she looked across the table and realized Sioned was sitting there looking awfully amused. She had quite forgotten he was there in her reverie.

"What's so funny, Elf?" She spat at him. He didn't even try to hide his humorous reaction to her obvious misconception. "If you are going to think it, keep it clean?"

He chuckled then at her very obvious anger. "There, there Tiger!" He knew he was infuriating her to the boiling point. Elves were capricious that way. "So, what are we going to do about Gria?"

She had hoped he would go away when ignored. She pushed her hair back in exasperation, took a deep breath to steady her raw nerves.

"Well, how can I possibly do anything to help you magical creatures find another magical creature that doesn't want to be found?" She eyed him with incredulity.

"You have the technology to locate her energy, Endarra." Sioned had leaned forward to emphasize his desire that she take him seriously. She knew better than to piss him off in retaliation. Elves *always* won those matches of wit. Of course, they had a few centuries on everyone else.

"Just as you can detect the same energy signature, Sioned." She threw back dryly, wondering why he didn't.

He shook his head in denial, "Not when we don't want it to be detected. But there is nothing we can do about our body heat as opposed to our energy signature which is soul, Endarra."

Realizing he was not up to tricks, Endarra thoughtfully took a big drink of her cherished coffee. She had obtained quite a store of this from the space pirates she had run across a few years ago. It was her prized and guarded hoard and she only allowed herself a cup on very special occasions.

The galley crew were good about preparing it at those times. She reached for the cup again but Doon beat her to it. Her knife was at his throat before it touched his lips.

A roaring laugh broke from him as he gave her the cup and pushed the knife away. He slid into the remaining seat with his plate.

Endarra stood, taking a last gulp from the cup, leaving a mouthful for Doon, she placed it by his plate with a wink. "Just enough to make you want more, lover!" She chuckled as she walked away. "You coming, Sioned?" Dropping her plate off at the exit, they headed for the control room.

Doon watched ruefully. *There went that opportunity.*

After an hour of searching, Sioned and Endarra agreed that Gria would not be attending the life-giving ceremony called *Siren Song*. There were enough others, but each would give up a little more life energy than anticipated.

Knowing Gria's selfishness and her capriciousness well, it was a toss-up as to which motivated her at the moment, but she would answer to them all when she returned.

CHAPTER TWO

Tarian, Owena and Gareth were the first onsite, on the *center cross* in the lay lines of Enceladus. They were fairly buzzing with anticipation. They were doing something never done before.

Having scouted the area and determined nothing sentient existed here, they checked out the corals and crystals growing on Kyra's floor. Right where they were to perform their feat.

The corals had natural indents that were smooth. Like giant clam shells. Perfect for holding Maben.

Thermonuclear vents among the corals created a perfect flow of warm water rising up and flowing back down in lotus pattern, keeping a warm buffer between the corals and the cooler ocean water.

Actually, Kyra had very little of what could be called *cold water*. Heat generated from its core and a little rose to the top, just under the crust and was held there also creating a buffer between the top of Kyra and the crust.

However, the water was, otherwise, lifeless. Nearly dead.

Nothing lived here that they were not bringing with them. That they knew of, that is.

They needed to give the moon life. Magic was their venue, and a gift from Mekhyr, of Titan & the other Fallen Angels.

For the purpose of planting something he had entrusted to Gareth. Something that must not be unsealed yet but must be moved deep into the core. Once there they could unseal the package.

The fairies and elves poured out of the airlock with air breathers. There would be no talking, and this would take up to a full day. They could not be interrupted to change air packs for the bubbles.

Muir-Gheilt were set free from all the ships, with lights from those ships bathing the area, enough to mimic daylight for miles.

Tail colors flashing as they undulated through the water. Trinkets around their necks flashed brilliant colors, too.

They were an amazing show all by themselves. Working out the kinks in unrestrained aerobics. She could have watched them just like this for the rest of time. Mesmerized.

Then the real show started. A subtle glow at first then shimmering, thrumming colors filled with all the sounds of the universe. Weaving and waving as those using the magic hummed and spent the energy they had. Slowly, ever so slowly leaching it out to the object. Pushing it into the floor of the ocean. Deeper and deeper, building energy to a crescendo as they prepared to unseal the casing.

The entire day passed. Watchers went and returned several times. Always on edge, knowing they may miss the main event if they didn't hurry.

She had just returned from such a foray to the restroom when the humming stopped, and a ball of energy condensed from the magic they had been using, shooting straight up toward the surface and then it swooped forcefully into the hole made.

As it connected with the case, the slam was equivalent to a small nuclear bomb and the force of it threw the group back several hundred yards. The energy pushed the ships along the ocean's bottom, almost as far.

It was dark at first. After the blast. Then, an agonizingly impossible beautiful glow, full of every color in existence sprayed out into the water.

Falling here and there, the flares of light became hardened brilliantly hued crystals. Basking everything in the glorious light. The colors melted into the soon to be coral maben beds.

The water shimmered and flowed, pushing ever further into the deep dark. Replacing the dank and lifeless water that would soon cease to exist.

The scene erupted into rampant emotion, wild and raw. Muir-Gheilt flashed through the lifegiving water, celebrating arrival and their new home.

White faced and drained, elves and fae folk trooped back onto the ships through the airlocks, handing off their breathers and heading for their rooms.

Events were unfolding rapidly now. With the Muir-Gheilt now oceanside, that left the maben in makeshift shipside ponds, until the beds were complete.

And the rest? A handful of ships crews and those Titans and Varrain chosen to assist on the airside of the domes as they went.

Titans were tech wizards. Somehow bred into them. Only a handful had volunteered for the journey.

They knew it was a one-way ticket and though they had families, they sacrificed themselves for the sake of the masses who would one day need to make their own journey.

There was a mass exodus of rooms as everyone headed for the common room for the feast. They were having the delicacy of delicacies, Horned Breen, roasted on a spit in the *big* kitchen.

Breen were like miniature cows of earth according to Mekhyr. Succulent and nourishing.

There was a rumor going round that there was only enough for one serving and only a handful didn't want to be first in line.

Especially when they smelled the gravy ladled onto slabs of meat that sizzled in their own juices. The fruity and savory sauces for the accompanying vegetation and fish emitted mouthwatering odors.

They had pretty much survived on mushy combinations of the latter and fillers of packaged meals since leaving Titan.

Dinner tonight consisted of a tiny sliver of a fragment of the stock they brought for the livestock and farm domes.

The party lasted several hours and by the time the last person headed for his room, it was only three hours until they were scheduled to begin work. Others were just beginning their work and would sleep in the morning.

Oceanside, Muir-Gheilt couples and their families floated in tight groups with the aid of a trophin. A special seaweed used for this purpose now and then but eaten more often than not.

They brought plenty of the roots to plant in their new abode. Not to mention a plentiful store of woven dried weed for just this purpose until they could grow the filigreed floor domes.

They were all tethered to coral, completely sated and peaceful in their newly made home.

Endarra watched, sleepless. Restless in her plans for the morrow.

Missing Doon who was going over a stack of vellums with the Titans, making last minute decisions regarding the dome layout.

He moved one from the outer edges, setting it finally near the center of the ship in the core ring that had previously acted as *just* a corridor. "It makes more sense to put the farm within reach of the kitchens, yes?" He raised an eyebrow at the techies. "Then there is the whole carbon / oxygen thing, right." He grinned knowing he had won the argument. They had already decided to centrally vent to the surface through the center shaft of each city dome.

Cairbre hung his head. The Head Technician had worked the whole trip to present a perfect layout. "Well, I think you are right." Pursing his lips as though thoughtful, seeking to hide the dejected feeling that threatened to overwhelm him. Couldn't command much respect acting like that.

Doon cleared his throat. "But look at the amazing job you did, Cairbre. I see nothing else that I would change." Nodding at Cairbre he let his honest admiration shine through.

Cairbre perked up and smiled. "Appreciated, Doon!" He motioned his assistants to document the changes and follow them to the water.

Doon thought for the umpteenth time that he felt such love for Endarra, as they headed to the airlock. He wished to marry her. Ergo the mission.

He stopped at their corridor. "I'll be out in a minute." Cairbre inclined his head in acknowledgement and continued down the hall.

They were notified, before departure, the current rules of life did not apply anymore for them. They were to develop their own rules. Rules that applied to their new society in a new place.

They still had to appoint a council to work strictly on the laws of life. That would benefit all and encourage a peaceful, productive population.

It would take time to fine tune it, but they had a solid base from which to start. He passed the team heading out to seed the ocean with a variety of plants and simple organisms in anticipation of the release of their final tanks. The ones containing the fish.

Briggia had informed them this release should happen within a couple weeks. The new growth would take a while longer, so they would need a temporary oceanside lacy dome big enough to give them ample room, so they could keep the precious stock of fish fed and healthy.

They would start on this after their layout for the big dome.

CHAPTER THREE

Cairbre led his prestigious Techie Elite group past the airlock as he stepped out. Baari, Engoldo, Daria, Faryen, Hamarre, Diarmond, Grodna, Opria, Logori, Conn & Brighid nodded their heads at Doon as they followed.

Hamarre, Diarmond, Logori and Conn were Titan, Engoldo was elf and the rest were Muir-Gheilt.

They held glass sheets with portions of the vellum layout embedded. A couple carried collapsible stands for the sheets.

They began placing them around the area of the first dome. Soon the Techies and engineers had gathered around the stands to discuss their part in the job ahead. This was an outlying dome connected to Rashidan by a tunnel.

A little growling and a lot of hand movements later, they dispersed, working their way toward the Muir-Gheilt setting the foundation.

This was one for history. They watched as the merfolk swept the area flat with their powerful tails then formed a ring around it.

Dancing with primal instinct, chanting a tune only their throats could form, the sand suddenly began to glow red then became translucent glass many yards thick.

The odd thing was the lack of heat. Everyone knew you had to heat sand to form glass. But apparently somebody forgot to notify the merfolk of that fact.

Then the fascinating thing was the clarity as one looked down at sand that lay below the glass. Odd and disconcerting. The young would love it! Doon kind of liked the feeling of openness.

Sand was *summoned* with a wave of a hand and began to form the curved walls. Fittings were installed by the engineers as the wall was created.

It was choreographed precision that allowed one to feel as though the wall did not exist. Glass benches were built in. They would later be fitted with soft cushions.

Cairbre, always watchful, called out to Diarmond and Opria, "Hey, could you two wait until we are done here?" Opria winked back at him, "If you weren't looking you wouldn't be concerned, now would ya?"

Diarmond chuckled at her quick wit and delivery. Just enough to make it sting and enough humor to soothe.

He grabbed her around her delightfully tiny waist and swung her around into a kiss that made her release the sexiest guttural sound from the back of her throat.

Opria pushed him away, mockingly irritated at the grins and stares. Go, do what you do best, beast! Hard labor!"

She flashed her tail mesmerizingly as she slowly swam away. Grinning, once she passed the last engineer, Opria disappeared around a ship.

Cairbre shook his head, playfully registering disgust. Those Muir-Gheilt had a completely different set of moral rules. Pretty much it was, do what you want unless it hurts someone.

Though he had to admit that at least they now found isolated areas to be intimate. On Titan that is. Here, those spaces needed to be created.

There was the deep dark as the dark area outside the lights was dubbed. They had discovered there was now one fen-male missing from the other group. Quite possibly into that deep dark. Endarra confirmed it was his Fen-Folk liaison Beirnan who had gotten lost in an effort to scout for resources in their territory.

Endarra had received notice just prior to their day starting. The news was for those in leadership positions only. So they could avert potential disaster should he show up here.

Few even realized the Fen-Folk were here. It would be more difficult to keep them separate if they suddenly began showing up willy nilly. The Empagosans were hesitant about sending them but couldn't bring themselves to leave them to rot on Titan, nor could they destroy them outright. But they *could keep them isolated and let them naturally die off on Enceladus.*

"Hamarre, how about a hand over here?" The words came out a little gruff as he sympathized with them. They had no privacy since leaving Titan. Many, like Opria/Muir-Gheilt and Diarmond/Titan, were married.

There were a few promised couples as well. Such *interspecies* unions were accepted on Titan but not encouraged and supported.

The anatomy was very similar, though that of Muir-Gheilt retracted in males and didn't show on females. Otherwise, everything functioned the same and was discrete in the merfolk, even birth.

He had watched one of those a few years back. Forever etched in his mind, it was amazing to watch the little tyke slither right out of her belly.

There, at the bottom of their stomach was a resealable slit that was virtually invisible until needed.

It was equally fascinating to watch that opening just suck in and disappear. As Titan babies were always born as whatever DNA was not Titan, the intermarriages were creating more and more Muir-Gheilt.

Sadly, the magic in unmixed Muir-Gheilt, was not passed on in full, to mixed maben. Eventually it would die out altogether as the blood line became less pure. Though it would take considerably longer than the Fen-Folk. Many hundreds of generations in fact.

Mekhyr seemed oddly happy about that. Cairbre had always wondered about his reaction. Especially after he had looked into Mekhyr's lab once, when he, Cairbre was but a child.

He had watched Mekhyr remove something from the base of a Muir-Gheilt's neck after an accident had caused the magnificent beauty to perish.

It was immediately deposited into a glass vial and placed into the stasis chamber. It contained thousands of identical vials. *What was that?*

He had watched as the contents swirled and danced and glowed with the whitest light he had ever seen. He shook his head as though to clear it of the images.

"Hey Baari, I think we want that on the opposite side." Cairbre headed to his site. Baari always did get things backwards.

Baari obliged by moving the equipment to the other side of the new maben beds.

He was a great healer but not so much on engineering and Cairbre was a little too terrified of what he might see inside the one merwoman Baari had operated on. Granted it was just to remove a tumor and stitch her up but still!

CHAPTER FOUR

The fairies and elves had vanished after gathering enormous amounts of the mountains of glowing crystals. These were loaded onto water sleds and the little group just walked into the dark. Blinking out as they went.

There was some concern that they may become lost, but their one *little craft* was not unloaded yet and the big ships had enough for one more lift off and landing, in the event an evacuation was necessary. Obviously, the only option was to walk or swim.

It would take a few decades to fashion the larger propulsion systems out of raw crystal, even the turbo charged kind they had here. The little craft was limitless but didn't hold much.

Engoldo led the group toward the Fen-Folk encampment with the help of a compass. They lit their way with the crystals which they dropped on each side of their path as they walked to light their way back.

They would collect them on the return trip. It was an uneventful trek with one exception.

Beirnan, the fenman was lost in the dark for over forty-eight hours with no food. He was hearing echo from two directions. Almost midway between the two encampments though hundreds of miles apart.

With nothing to absorb or redirect the sounds, he simply became disoriented and was no longer sure what he should do. Finally deciding to go toward the loudest.

To his benefit, he quickly realized. He was soon aggressively leading Engoldo's party in the other direction. Maybe Fen-Folk were slower than Muir-Gheilt, but they still had some magical prowess in the water.

He was soon back with word that they were nearly to the first encampment. Another day's march. Then he disappeared in the direction of home.

Engoldo had anticipated he would, but wasn't concerned. They were going to rest for a few hours and proceed later.

The fairies were surrounding them with a magically *sand spun* protective net with opening, comprised of unbreakable glass strands. It would serve two purposes.

Keeping them from floating away as well as protecting them from any marauding bands of Fen-Folk.

Fairies were good to have along. They glow so helped provide another light source for the trip as an added bonus.

CHAPTER FIVE

Logori watched as the engineers filed back in through the airlock. Tired and hungry, they headed for the communal area first.

Some grabbing a quick meal and heading back to their quarters with it. Others filing past the buffet and still others giving orders for the meals they wanted, content to wait while resting.

Turned out the buffet was leftovers from their feast. Just as good the second time around. "Hey Cairbre," Logori headed toward his friend's table. "Feel like company?"

"Sure, have a seat," Cairbre pushed back the chair with his foot. "How are you? You look beat."

"Not bad", Logori grinned. "We'll get used to the pace. How about you? You were really pushing it out there." He sat with his plate and cup. Sighing, he took a big swig of the tea. Nice.

"When are we going to have our first meeting?"

Cairbre shrugged. "Probably after we get the first dome city done and fully functional. About a month?"

Logori nodded, "Reasonable timing." He knew they could do it if they pushed as hard as Cairbre had today. He also knew their ship supplies would run out in about six months.

Hopefully the farming and ranching would be in full swing by then. So three months of growing and they would have fresh food with poultry and fish. There would even be dairy in restricted amounts.

Cairbre watched the wheels turn in his friend's head. "Have you been recording the things you would like to see in our new home?"

"Actually, yeah. Isn't everyone?" Logori raised an eyebrow.

"Well, they were asked to but not everyone is capable of the imagination it takes, Logori. You know that." He chided his friend. "Which is why I made sure you were on the roster for this mission."

Logori looked up in surprise. "Didn't know that." He mumbled, embarrassed. Cairbre laughed.

"Well, it's true and there is good reason to believe you can run the committees." He laughed again when Logori looked up in alarm. "Oh no. I don't think that's a good idea, Cairbre!" He started to scoot his seat back.

Cairbre reached out and placed a hand on Logori's arm. "Hold on a second. You have all the qualifications. Nobody else does and is free to work on this as a coordinator or leader."

He looked solidly into Logori's eyes, knowing he would have to give in for the good of the whole. He was not disappointed.

Logori sat back finally. "I don't know the first thing about running meetings, Cairbre." He spread his fingers, palms up in supplication.

He knew he must but surely there was an outline or instructions. Cairbre grinned. "Not a problem. Let's go have a look at the library after we eat."

Tucking into their food, they were soon in the corridor and nearing the library which held the entire Titan database from every system, not only from Titan, but from every known inhabited rock in the Universes and then some.

Of course, much was in other languages, though apparently, there was an auto translator on board. One could request the data printed, digital or verbal. Nice!

Even nicer was the program Cairbre pulled up on the 3 D screen in the middle of the room.

"How about a program with the ability to function as a prototype? This computer is the best creation anywhere has to offer." He looked over at Logori.

Logori walked around the screen image, "How does it work?" He was intrigued.

Cairbre spoke, "Inlivia! Ten domes, twenty-five miles across each, with 1000-foot tunnels between them. Northbound." The room lit up with screen activity. A to-scale miniature took shape, replacing the screen.

Logori grinned, catching on quickly, as Cairbre knew he would. "Inlivia! Population twenty-three fairies, twelve elves, ninety Titans, one hundred and thirty Fen-Folk, three thousand four hundred and seventeen Muir-Gheilt: make seventeen hundred seventy-six male, sixteen hundred forty-one female.

Of those make eight hundred thirty-one juveniles and three hundred and three maben.

The animated beings rapidly populated the domes and surrounding area. They moved as though living life from moment to moment.

Logori was completely enamored of the scene before him. His very own universe, full of life. The rush of adrenaline and potential were overpowering.

"Inlivia! Dome society half patriarchal, half matriarchal." Inlivia raced through her data banks searching out a similar circumstance with similar beings in those quantities and the life in the domes took on an entirely different pattern. Different clothing, mannerisms and lifestyles.

"Inlivia! Basic laws," he hesitated briefly, "from earth 1855." He had chosen a timeframe contrasting to the society in place to see what would happen.

Inlivia supplied the voices of the denizens in the scene. Court proceedings were in play. Women were being tried for assorted reasons. They were losing ground to patriarchal law.

"Inlivia! Save for later as file enceladus_society_potential." Inlivia obliged and as the last item disappeared, Logori followed Cairbre out into the hall. "I'll see you later Cairbre." He grinned, "Glad you talked me into this. See you tomorrow same time?"

Cairbre shook his head, "Sorry Logori, you're on your own now. Inlivia saved your voice print for security so you will be the only one who can access your file. Can't wait to see what you make of it!"

He clapped Logori on the shoulder, smiling with confidence and they headed out the airlock to look around before turning in.

CHAPTER SIX

Balor stood looking out at the new maben beds. The young ones were tethered in with the multipurpose seaweed fronds that were also planted in and around the beds.

Opria's twins were playfully pushing each other and tugging on the fronds around them. Diarmond swiftly covered the space between them just in time to catch little Kyne as his tether broke.

He let him get a head start then raced after him, catching Kyne as Rylee burst into laughter at the sight.

It was actually a pretty fair race as Diarmond's legs slowed him considerably.

Clapping her chubby little hands as her tail kept her in place, Rylee chortled, "Me, Daddy, me." She reached out, melting his heart at the innocent, trusting love in her eyes.

He would have to sleep near them until a juvenile dome was created.

It wouldn't be long until they would be old enough to either tether as the adults did to sleep or to spin a mineral and sand lattice dome. Muir-Gheilt grew quickly. Approximately ten Titan years to adulthood.

He hugged them close, kissing each in the crease of their tiny necks while they wriggled trying to escape the tickling. Good thing he was wearing a breather instead of a bubble. He shook with inner laughter. Opria watched lovingly from the shadows.

She was part of the team dealing with the necessary *other* areas. Deep sea composting was a real challenge. Thank goodness for the oceanside vids Endarra had ordered for them.

Watching her husband and children together was more rewarding than anything else life had to offer.

It was past time to get a bite to eat and sleep. She took one last long look and began to thrash around, trying to scream as she was grabbed from behind.

Feeling the turmoil in the water, Diarmond glanced up sharply. This was, after all, a new ocean. Did they know everything about it?

He swam closer to the general location the swirling came from. His eyes were limited in the darkness. Seeing nothing, Diarmond headed back toward the babes.

Rylee raced past him heading into the dark, arms wide open, "Momma", she yelled gleefully.

Diarmond just managed to catch her by the tail as she streaked by.

Baari was close on her fin but didn't stop, eyes on something in the distance, and it hit Diarmond that Rylee was reaching out to her Mom!

Heart pounding in his chest as others joined Baari, Diarmond hugged little Rylee close to his chest.

Kyne floated expectantly above his bed on his back, tail fin above his chubby little face as he grasped it, laughing.

Balor and his security team swam by with breathers on. There would be no need for verbal communication.

They were armed from head to toe. Grodna led them, tail flashing so fast he flew by, a blur of color.

All fighters and Muir-Gheilt wore net bags at their waists. One for food and one for the glowing crystals they had gathered. One or two others hung empty, just in case they were needed.

He heard a scream and knew it was Opria. Heart quaking, he held Rylee even closer and she began to pound his chest with tiny fists, struggling to break free.

Beirna pried him loose from the precious little maben and tethered her next to her brother again.

Taking the precaution of using three tethers this time. One on each wrist and one on her tail.

She threw herself into making sure the maben were all safe. A bottle here and a loose tether there. She was soon satisfied that the tykes were none the worse for whatever was happening.

She had called earlier for a fresh crew of maben tenders. As they arrived and chose sections of the maben beds, she swam to Diarmond.

He noticed she was there, and it was good to know someone understood his pain and fear.

It was better that he remain and let the others deal with this.

Though it strained him to the core to sit by, he was not Muir-Gheilt. Neither was he a trained security staff member. He was an engineer and knew well his own weaknesses.

He would be a danger to his beloved rather than a help, by getting in the way.

Doon joined him. "Diarmond, buddy, I need you to help in the control room. We can track but need your computer expertise to utilize the program."

Diarmond stood silent a moment, letting the words sink in through the haze enveloping his brain. He *could* help. Of course he could.

"Diarmond," Doon called as he raced to keep up with Diarmond who was heading toward the ship. "Wait for me buddy!"

Once in the control room, Diarmond brought the 3D screen up, "Inlivia! Perimeter 1000 miles." He well knew the speed capabilities of the Muir-Gheilt. By now they would be approaching even this line.

"Inlivia! Show heat sources." Inlivia showed all the sources of extreme heat first. All the thermonuclear cones and then there they were.

Fine, barely visible streaks in the darkness, one stood out in contrast to the others. He wondered how that could be as all the merfolk registered the same temperatures.

Surely there was a glitch in the program. He would have to see to it Cairbre calibrated the sensors.

Using the radio, he tuned it to the security frequency, "Balor, they are 500 miles ahead of you. Nothing you guys can do. Come on back." It took a minute, but they watched as that group turned. They watched as another, larger object flew past Balor's group.

Endarra! In the small craft. Diarmond gave a short sigh of relief as the constriction around his heart eased slightly. She must have had it supercharged.

She had the same radar system onboard as they were using. She gained on the farthest streaks faster than any of the Muir-Gheilt could go. Well, with the exception of Opria.

It suddenly hit him how vulnerable they all were. Here in this strange place. Were they absolutely sure there were only Muir-Gheilt and Fen-Folk here in this vast ocean?

Suddenly they saw a tiny dot flitting around the small craft. Nobody here had a single doubt that they were watching Gria on radar.

None of the other fairies bothered to interact with them much, though they did love to spin stories now and again. For some reason Gria had decided they were all fascinating.

However, they were whimsical creatures and he didn't know if she would help Endarra or the *others,* whatever or whoever they were.

Or if she would just simply grab Opria and bring her back. Then again, she might abandon the whole thing.

Most of all he wondered how she got there and *why*? Everyone had been looking for her a couple days ago. Maybe she had seen something and followed it. Fairies could be like that.

The radar began to flicker. A burst of heat radiated from the center of the group with Opria. For a moment there was nothing.

Then the craft, dot and larger streak turned back. The pale ones stayed as they were. It was obvious by the time they were half way back that the small craft had one in its grasp, via the long arm and metal claw.

Come on guys, let's be there to greet them. They have one of the kidnappers.

When the little party arrived, Diarmond grabbed his wife around the waist and swung her round and round. Ecstatic to find her safely returned to him.

Gria simpered and bowed to all the happy thanks and whistles from the males gathered around the small craft. She made her way sleepily to her quarters.

Tomorrow she would tell her side of the story. For tonight, there was Endarra's.

Endarra wasn't disappointed as she watched the faces through the front glass of the craft.

She raised the craft arm and opened the claw.

A creature resembling the octopi of earth fell out and began to swing its tentacles in panic.

CHAPTER SEVEN

Doon acted quickly to contain the many armed creature. Tethering one arm as his team tethered others. Not with the usual frond but with rope made of the same.

They managed to secure enough of it to drag it writhing in anger and fear to an outer holding compartment created for the Muir-Gheilt.

For some yet undetermined reason this species did not mimic its earther counterpart in producing *ink*, however it did have a mouth which one or two lucky ones managed to avoid at the last moment.

Closing the door, they could see it through the portal. Thrashing violently against its cage.

Balor made his way to the middle of the crowd. "Listen up everyone."

He waited as they quieted. "Until we can control this thing and its buddies, everyone is to stay within well-lit areas and never be alone.

I want everyone to travel around in triples or quadruples. Keep weapons handy. Everyone carries a long blade."

He let that sink in. "We need a team to make sure the path to the waste station is clearly and brightly lit for at least five hundred yards on each side of the path."

Several volunteers headed for the crystals they had piled into a small mountain. It was as large as a ship.

Each little crystal glowed with enough light to cover a four-square yard area with the brilliance of sunlight, fading out to an area ten times that.

Using a transport net, they created a safe zone with as many as they could carry at one time and began developing the path.

In the meantime, they were to use the shipside privies.

Endarra, having put the small craft away, headed for Gria's quarters. She owed an explanation for her disappearance. She owed a bigger one regarding the creatures she was with.

"Come in," Gria sat in a corner of her tiny chair musing over the circumstances of the last few hours.

She fluttered a hand in the air and her room became big enough for Endarra as she entered.

"What?" She yawned in a parody of boredom. Endarra grinned at the fairy. "Thanks for the extra space."

She looked around the normal room which, just seconds ago, she had seen was an opulent harem styled room with a warm pool in the center, judging by the steam.

She could have sworn she had seen a brownie or two waiting on her. *Were they allowed to bring those?*

She would have to check, though little good it would do as fairies were accountable to no one, other than when choosing to do as a Fallen Angel requested now and then.

She wondered briefly, where did she keep them? Nobody had mentioned any pranks or missing items. Maybe they were magically restrained.

"Nice digs," She finally said, nodding in appreciation. "Liked the previous one, too."

She really had. Somehow it appealed to the feminine in her and she wished she had just a fraction of that magic!

Gria looked her over, interested in the obvious appreciation. "Yeah, that's home. It's nice being able to recreate it."

Knowing that sounded like a brag, Gria smirked, checking out her immaculate nails. She felt like being snarky today. Those stupid creatures with all those waving arms tried to eat her friend, Opria.

Deciding she would rather be home, she changed the room back, keeping the larger size.

Endarra was getting dizzy with all this room changing and sizing. She realized even her attire had changed! Of all the nerve! She glared at Gria.

"Really? You couldn't ask me if, never mind, this will go nowhere fast." Endarra choked out, biting her tongue. This fairy could really tick her off.

Gria smiled. She really enjoyed getting to Endarra. So self-confident and capable yet always a step behind herself.

She sat at the edge of the pool dangling her feet in the water. "Come on." She waved Endarra over. "Enjoy." Tilting her head back Gria posed as provocatively as a fairy could.

Endarra wanted to laugh and didn't dare. All she needed was a lifetime of retribution. Fairies *never* forgot. "What the heck!" She sat down and swung her legs in.

"Awwww." Stress melted off in waves. "I can't believe how selfish you are, Gria! All this time we could have been living a life of luxury."

Gria laughed, "Even fairies have limits." Somehow making that admission of limitation sound like a jab. How did she always manage to do that?

"What do you think about those octopi?" Endarra was puzzled. "And why were you there? Aren't you afraid you could get lost?"

Gria swelled up until she was larger than everything in the room and back. "Questions?"

Endarra shook her head. "Show off!"

Gria smirked again. "Seriously though, I caught sight of one of them our first day here and followed as the group headed off. I didn't realize there were more hanging around.

The next group arrived with Opria just prior to your arrival."

Gria shrugged, "So I knocked them out and the rest is history." How is Opria, by the way?"

"Fine. Last I saw she was wrapped around that hunk of a husband she snagged. Kids were ok too."

She got up. "Time for me to crash. It was a long day!" She reached for the door panel. "See you later Gria." *So that's where Gria had got off to!*

She turned to smile and headed out into the hall, knowing that behind her the amazing room had become tiny again. Thankfully Gria had returned her clothing! She really could be considerate if not asked. Capricious as ever.

Well there was plenty to think about and do. They would have to send out a research team to investigate the indigenous denizens Gria had punched with her light magic. One question stuck out like a sore thumb. *Why didn't they see the energy signatures of these creatures previously? Oh, and why couldn't they find Gria?*

She would have to read ten operational manuals to erase the magical memories and get a renewed grip on normal life.

Maybe that was part of the reason fairies kept their distance. They were so very far beyond the scope of human reasoning that they appeared to be godlike in their abilities.

Even elves had some limitations, though on second thought, not many.

She had always known the two species had amazing power and had even seen some at work but never at the magnitude they had all witnessed here in Kyra.

Onboard, during the trip, they had been seen only rarely. Usually if needed in one department or another.

Most often it was the hydroponics and Muir-Gheilt needs that made them necessary.

She was looking forward to finishing those domes. Even one would probably hold everyone, maybe two.

A couple more to spread out and the rest could be developed over time.

She wondered if Doon had any time free tonight. Dinner would be nice. Maybe they would be lucky enough to have some private time and maybe snuggle through a movie.

She would ask Inlivia to locate some they could understand and enjoy.

Stopping at the galley she chose two meals, put them on a tray, *just in case.* She added some drinks and returned to the hallway.

Humming at the thought of a pleasant, stress free evening with someone she enjoyed.

CHAPTER EIGHT

Logori was anxious to get started on his new project. Hot tea and a breakfast snack in one hand and a sheaf of papers in another, he elbowed the door panel.

As the door slid into the wall, he entered and put everything on the console by the computer. "Inlivia! Bring up Enceladus society."

Taking a bite of the sandwich, he took a mouthful from the cup and mumbled, "Inlivia! Change laws to Titan 2033."

That was from a couple hundred years ago but times were good then and it was before the first gas geysers.

Inlivia quickly changed the laws and everything took on a more normal and comfortable aspect. "Inlivia! Show me text history for Andromeda Galaxy from one thousand years ago. Make it societal rules."

Cairbre stuck his head in the door and grinned at the sight. Withdrawing he headed for the airlock. Today was going to be very productive.

As the engineers had already laid out the first three domes along with the main dome of Rashidan and connecting tunnels, complete with flooring, benches and other fixtures they were ready to finish the domes now.

Today they would manufacture the shatterproof, high impact ceiling and wall glass. The entire population was turning out to watch.

This was even more intricate than the previous work as every detail of every room would go into place evenly paced with raising the walls.

In a twenty-five-mile diameter!

Built into the walls were sensors that were controlled with remotes. The walls could turn dark and opaque or be invisible enough that merfolk would swim right into them.

Not nice but kind of funny he thought grinning.

Magic played a ninety-five percent part in the engineering of domes. They were all very grateful for the addition of the fairies and elves.

The Muir-Gheilt were, of course, capable of building their lacy domes but this type of building required all three species just as when they jump started the moon's energy.

That was focused and beyond stunningly dazzling. What was coming was as dazzling and brilliant but involved creating beyond the scope of most persons understanding.

The magic took on a whole new look and would be like a weeklong art show at some weeklong fireworks show bombarded with the most glorious crystalline dust in an array of colors that literally hurt one to view for long.

The engineers and Varrain had special eyewear though the Muir-Gheilt, elves and fairies needed no protection.

Those watching shipside had treated glass between them and the construction. Though only a few hours of work a day was possible, it was great entertainment for those starved for free time.

Personally, Cairbre would be in the thick of it so, for him it was work, though pleasant work.

And it was time for his day to begin, he mused as he watched the approach of the cadre of engineers and Doon with his team.

"Everyone ready to do some serious building on Rashidan?" He looked them over, confident that they were anxious to start.

They had decided on the city names and general layout prior to departure from Titan. Rashidan would house the Rulers of Enceladus when the others arrived.

"Engoldo." Have the Muir-Gheilt teams begun creating the walls?" He glanced at the leader of the elves.

"Yes, they started a few hours ago." He added thoughtfully, "We should still have plenty of help with the building today. Many of the Muir-Gheilt are experienced in this form of building. Besides, we need them to construct the inner domes for their use according to their requirements."

"Great, then let's go." He started for the airlock again, crew in tow. He looked over at Engoldo, "Are your added Muir-Gheilt ready to join us?"

"Absolutely! They have been on site for over an hour now, waiting." He smiled at Cairbre. He liked Cairbre.

Cairbre understood more than most and had such a pleasant attitude *all* the time.

He didn't seem to realize everyone was different. This made him an ally for anyone and more times than not, Cairbre could be seen mentoring or counseling. He had such a talent for it.

Cairbre was handsome where the females were concerned, tall and considerate. His deep voice seemed to really affect them and he knew how to flirt. Engoldo had seen *this* numerous times.

For some odd reason though, he was never *with* any of the females he flirted with, Engoldo reflected.

He made a mental note to determine why some day. He began to hum, looking forward to a day well spent.

Cairbre raised an eyebrow and chuckled inwardly as he listened to the tune. It was reminiscent of days Cairbre had only seen in earth movies but Engoldo had lived it in person.

Nice music they had then. It had a distinct Gaelic lilt.

They came up to the other teams and spread out to begin their work.

CHAPTER NINE

Gria mumbled and turned in her bed of, softer than air, down. Her dreams carried her far into the past when she was but a babe.

Green hills and meandering streams. Giant trees and the ancient homes built into their trunks and among their supportive branches.

Twilight had been her favorite time of day. When pixies and brownies came out and everyone danced under the stars.

Pipers played and some sang. Glorious nights with a sky full of diamonds. She had been sure it would last forever.

She did, but *it* did not. It seemed only a fleeting time ago that they had been transported to Titan and then here to Enceladus.

She turned again, seeing her parents and siblings in their home. It was one of the rare ones that wound in and out of the center oak in their village.

Her room had been located near the tree's top. She enjoyed flying to the balcony after an evening out with friends.

The timid pixie peeked around the bedpost and curtains to see if Gria had awakened yet. Pixies were *never* timid but Gria's temper and the lack of anywhere else to go had them all traumatized.

She darted out of the room and to the fully stocked kitchen. "You have time but if I were you I would hurry faster than you are!"

She nodded her head sharply for emphasis and tapped her foot anxiously as she eyed the head brownie, Shari.

Shari glared at the pixie. There had always been antagonism between the two species. Pixies were so *ignorant and silly.* She shrugged her off and turned to the stove.

"Hurrying as fast as I can!" She looked over her shoulder, "Now leave me be so I can finish without your *attitude!"* she snapped.

Tressa yawned, doing her best to look uninterested. "I'll go wherever I want to go and when I want to." She studied her fingernails in an insolent manner.

"Now!" Shari turned on Tressa and brandished a wooden spoon above her head. "Before I smack you, you impudent bug!"

That triggered a glare from Tressa finally and she pouted as she turned to return to Gria's room. "Can't say I didn't warn you, stain!" She shot back smugly. She knew well how aggravated Brownies got when connected with underwear.

She was rewarded when the spoon flew past her head to hit the wall in the next room. She laughed tauntingly.

"Oh, if I could get my hands on that glittery piece of shiny dust called Tressa." Shari growled, thinking of the things she would do to her.

She finished plating the meal and covered it. "Kila, come here and take this up to Gria."

"Do I have to, Shari? It's so heavy!" Tears welled up in her pretty, overly large eyes.

"That isn't going to work on me, Kila." Shari snorted her displeasure and thrust the tray into the recalcitrant young brownie's hands. "Now don't drop this."

Kila headed for the stairwell. It was too heavy to allow pixies to fly it to the room, so it naturally fell on the younger brownies to do.

She absolutely detested this chore. If brownies had even a fraction of pixie magic, there would be a few changes made around here!

The only magic they possessed were by-products of fairy magic, such as the glowing crystals. Gria wouldn't even indulge them with a tiny bit of dust to help them wait on her.

Just a few grains would allow her to fly the trays up. Mean, selfish, self-centered, ugly, stupid fairy! She felt better then, and the tray felt just a little bit lighter.

Then her conscience bit her and she realized how nasty mean she was being even thinking such terrible things. Gria rubbed off on her more times than she cared to admit.

For the zillionth time, Kila wondered if they would ever be free of Gria and the other fairies.

The stairs culminated in the aerie open to dappled sunlight, an invisible magic net inhibiting any intrusions.

It warmed her brownie heart to feel so free for this was the closest she was allowed to it. This was only a false glamour after all.

Even if she wasn't magically bound to these rooms, they were miles from the surface of a crusty ocean in space. There were no trees or sunlight. For the moment, however, she could imagine home again.

It was little wonder that Gria preferred to remain in her quarters when she could enjoy a life like this. Ever true to herself, she *did* enjoy comfort and freedom.

Kila wondered if she had disappeared during the life-giving ceremony so she could keep her power intact.

The sun in this glamour was moving even as she reflected on these things and she heard Gria stirring in her bed.

She hurried forward with the tray. "Good morning, ma'am." If she wasn't so loaded down she would curtsey. She hoped Gria would not notice.

CHAPTER TEN

Briggia threw down the wrench. A few choice words later, she kicked it across the room and sat on the stool next to the air cleaning system.

Well, it was a good thing this was only one of many, but she wasn't happy about losing the use of even one as it meant one less for the cities.

Surely, she could find another part in a storage locker on one ship or another. There were duplicates of nearly everything needed to survive on Enceladus.

She could manufacture one if she could get her hands on a replicator. Oh, and the raw materials to feed it with, she thought sarcastically.

"Well that was helpful!" Balor laughed as he watched her jump. "What has you in a snit, Briggia?"

She laughed ruefully, "The central air scrubber in this unit is bad." She opened another panel, looking for spare parts that might have been left on site. Nothing!

"Have you called any of the other ships?" He raised an eyebrow and hid a grin.

She was sure funny when she was flustered but if you thought the wrench was treated badly, try going against her by laughing!

Briggia looked up suspiciously. "I heard that, Balor!" She went in search of the abused wrench.

"Heard what?" He was careful not to antagonize her so what was she talking about?

"That laugh under your words, that's what." She smacked him on the head as she returned the wrench to the toolbox.

He reached up, grateful she smacked him with her hand and not the wrench! "Sis, knock it off!"

"I tried." This time she laughed. "So, what are you up to today, brother dearest?" She turned back to the panel. "There! I got it to work again. Not sure for how long though."

"Let's go get some breakfast, Sis." He smiled. "Got to bounce some ideas off someone. Might as well be a goofball like you."

Balor walked out laughing as she pretended she was going to throw the wrench again. *Sometimes!*

She put the panel back in place and hurried to catch up. "So, what's on your mind little brother?" It was fun to watch his face when she called him little.

He smirked, "Yeah, who's little?" He looked down two feet into her face. "I think you are the shor-tee here!"

She just shook her head, resigned to always losing to him. Her tummy grumbled. "Sorry. Hungry." They grabbed trays and loaded up. Both were hearty eaters.

Looking around, Balor caught sight of an empty table and steered Briggia in that general direction.

As they sat down with their meals, Briggia wriggled an eyebrow at her brother, "What's on your mind?"

"Well, as you know we have no ruler here. Nobody seems to be thinking about that, but we should. Before someone *decides* to take charge. Right?"

She began paying attention at the word ruler, "Yeah. But who?" She was starving. Deciding she could be rude to her own brother, she began digging in to the pile of food.

"I'm pretty sure Sioned could handle it and wouldn't try to retain the honor when they do finally arrive." He began inhaling the mountain of food on his plate.

"Sioned could what?" Sioned towered over them with his own tray of special food. Elves didn't eat meat of any kind. Dairy either. Balor turned red, "Rule us until the rest arrive." He looked earnestly at the lead elf. "What do you think, Sioned? Would you do this for us?"

"If I am voted in, yes. I will." He nodded before sipping at his cup. "Will you be setting the meeting, or do you want to ask Cairbre?" He peered at the two before him.

"Cairbre." Balor and Briggia stated simultaneously. Neither one willing to be in the limelight over something so controversial. Nobody would hold it against Cairbre!"

"Fine. Let me know what happens when I return." He picked his semi full tray up again and headed for his quarters. Breathing a sigh of relief, Balor grinned at Briggia. She just shook her head in awe. Her brother ought to be an ambassador or something.

As they finished eating, Briggia said, "Balor, why don't we go find Cairbre now. I think you are right. We need to settle this right away." She was concerned because Sioned immediately agreed and that elf never *immediately* agreed with *anything*! *And* he tried to hurry the meeting.

They finally located Cairbre twenty-five miles from the ships, at the far edge of Rashidan. They enlisted the aid of elf travel to get there quickly.

"Hi there Cairbre." Balor and Briggia chimed. They would *have* to stop doing that. They sounded like children.

Cairbre looked up in surprise from the instructions he was going over with Doon. "Hi back at you." He looked at them quizzically. "What brought you two all the way out here?"

"Be back in a minute," he told Doon and walked away with the visitors.

"Well, we need a leader," Balor spoke first. "Sioned is up for it if that tells you anything." He

looked Cairbre in the eye, "We don't dare let this become something so big that bad feelings will cause issues."

"Alright." He paused for a second, thinking. "Let's call it for tonight. Can you set it up? Say I'm calling it." He had realized as usual what the repercussions could be for them.

Doon radioed for an elf to come get them and they headed for communications. They could send out an area wide announcement.

CHAPTER ELEVEN

Progress was slow at the Fen-Folk encampment. Now that Beirnan was back with tales of the larger group and their section of ocean had become infused with life giving energy, the Fen-Folk relaxed and began settling in to their new home.

It soon became obvious that Beirnan was a great storyteller and the young surrounded him, drawing the curious elders into the group.

Brenin, the leader watched for a while, listening to the way the others were building and preparing and realized that his people also needed a purpose, or they would quickly transform into something like their voracious and nearly mindless ancestors.

Leaving them to their rest, he flashed through the water to the outermost reaches of the light crystals given them by the elves.

He had learned that the crystals came from the ground and were thought to have been created by the burst of energy from the "package". But Brenin knew better.

The Fen-Folk had always been miners of oceans and if there were any chance he was correct, he knew they would have a marketable skill that would provide them with trade goods.

Maybe the way of capitalism was difficult, but it was an ocean full of better than lazy degenerates getting into trouble with everyone or *eating* them.

Besides, there were necessities they had to obtain somehow and as there were pitiful few Fen-Folk compared to the Muir-Gheilt, the Fen-Folk must rely on the others for survival.

That just went against the fin. Fen-Folk were a proud folk who asked nobody for anything and this trip put a serious damper on that way of life!

On the way here, he had noticed the ship crossed an immense trench. That would be a great place to begin excavating.

When Brenin saw Beirnan leave the group he called him over. "When are you returning to the other side to study?"

Beirnan cocked his head quizzically at their leader, "In a couple more sleep cycles. Why?"

Brenin shook his head. "Don't really want to say why yet but we could sure use equipment to excavate with. Can you keep that much a secret for now?"

Beirnan nodded thoughtfully. "Sure. Want me to ask for a loan for a bit?" Relieved, Brenin nodded back. "Yep. Enough for a couple dozen to operate."

He swam away leaving Beirnan full of questions. Not one for idling, Beirnan gathered crystals into a small heap and began forming his "hut". Spinning the sand into glass designs.

This was one of only a handful of magical abilities shared with the Muir-Gheilt and it was more a result of what they were than what they were imbued with.

As he finished his little hut, thinking he would add more to it tomorrow, he glanced around and realized others had followed suit.

This was not unnoticed by Brenin who realized the value of harnessing the natural leadership qualities for his project.

As the last one finished his sleeping quarters, Brenin entered his own. He started his later than everyone else but had enough done to feel satisfied for the time being.

Brenin's story was a little different than the average fen. His mother carried an Empagosan gene, watered down by several generations. It caused his IQ to be elevated somewhat.

He suspected Beirnan had the same gene. *Ergo, tutoring by Mekhyr before leaving Titan so he could help the Fen-Folk adjust to Kyra.* Beirnan would be their liaison to the Fallen Angel.

Now if he could just encourage him to see his daughter, Aeres, he might have some amazing grandmaben.

Another result was a little more power in their magic. Who knew what they might achieve.

He drifted off to sleep, dreaming about the maben in his future.

Beirnan peeked out sensing everyone was sleeping. He rarely needed more than a couple hours. This gave him ample time to investigate the surrounding area. Grabbing a bagful of crystals, he began laying a path.

He played dumb, but he had observed Brenin's interest in the trench and with this new request, he was more than a little curious.

It took a third of the sleep cycle to arrive but once he looked into the depths, realizing the possibilities, he couldn't help himself.

If these light crystals came from the core of the little moon, who knew what other precious gems might be waiting for discovery.

An annoying escapee from the ships swam circles around his head, obstructing his view.

He snagged the fish and absentmindedly passed a hand over it, cooking it instantly, another perk to being fen, though most didn't bother, preferring sushi of the seas.

Eating it in a few bites, he threw the little carcass off to the side and descended into the blackness of the trench. He had enough crystals left in the bag at his waist to illuminate several hundred feet.

It seemed like forever before he noticed anything other than sand and rock. *What was that?*

He swam up for a closer look. There, in the crevice of that rock. *A glimmer of green flashed.* His eyes lit up and a slow grin spread across his handsome face.

He *knew* it! This moon wasn't as dead as everyone thought. Sure, it needed a major energy boost to enliven the water enough to support life as they knew it. But it also held treasure in its depths.

He drifted deeper, investigating every little crack and niche. There were more flashes of brilliant deep green hues and some lavender, ruby and indigo flashes as well.

Digging at one with a little trowel, tool of his trade, he unearthed larger gems but still no bigger than his thumb. There must be enormous mother lodes in here.

Whipping around to leave the little cave he had whittled out of the steep side, his tail hit the wall and he heard a deafening roar as the entire steep wall of the trough seemed to be falling in on him.

Choking and gasping for breath, Beirnan watched, horrified as the sand and rock formed around him, leaving no escape.

The trowel had fallen from his fingers as he raised his arms to shield his head and face. The only thing he retained was the bag of crystals.

He could very clearly see the newly formed sandy coffin he might very well die in and for the first time wished he had human legs with grasping toes to search for the trowel. Though little, it might have allowed him to dig a hole large enough for fresh water with precious air to get through.

But surely, they would be missing him when they awakened and would search for him. He flicked his tail back and forth, remaining upright though he could comfortably go horizontal to a point. It was a little terrifying thinking about accidentally hitting the sides again.

So, for two cycles, he refused to close his eyes. This was the second time in as many daily cycles that he had *gotten himself lost*. Would they even make the effort to locate him this time? After all, he had guided the troupe of elves and fairies back to them. He may well run out of air before they realized he had not gone to study.

Finally, he could not resist the lure of sleep, eyelids fluttering, he dreamed about the vast ocean and freely swimming in it.

CHAPTER TWELVE

Logori tapped his fingers lightly on the edge of the counter holding the computers. He had been going over records from the Gleia System and was impressed with the society they had grown into.

It had taken them a bit longer than it should have to arrive there but when they did, everything fell nicely into place.

A society free of violence on the scale seen in Earth's imaginative future vids. Free of infectious diseases, they were a long-lived lot. Mental illness was unheard of and they were leaders in the space trade.

They brought subtle guidance to many of the outlying Galaxies, many eons more primitive, some of them, than the Gleians had sprung from.

They seemingly, had a sense of the balance required to grow in a positive direction and Logori was convinced their "interferences" saved at least one Galaxy full of warring factions from extinction.

"Inlivia! Use final societal stage of Gleian growth in file Enceladus society." He sat back and watched as the scene sprang to life in the center of the room.

This never ceased to amaze him. It was only due to his humble spirit that he did not feel the power of this but instead felt more humbled by the challenge, knowing the society they would build depended on him getting this right.

It did concern him that he could not foresee what they would contribute to life outside their new home.

Surely, they could import something of value and develop that into something with substantially more value to the Universe. *But what?*

He shook his head, musing a moment more on the subject before switching to the scene before him. Until they learned more about this moon they were on, he was flying blind on the subject.

He spent the last few cycles inputting the personalities and idioms of the people he had travelled here with. It was interesting to see the paradigm shift with each new set of data.

Uh-Oh! He watched feeling a touch of dismay as the denizens of his imagination began to turn just a tad ugly toward one another.

What caused that? This whole business was more work than he had anticipated but the excitement of creating such a thing far outweighed the upsets.

He was learning much about the intricacies of interaction between those able to process thought and simple computer-generated lifeforms.

He hesitated before making another change. The last thing he wanted to do was unsnarl a messy societal knot.

It occurred to him that perhaps intelligence needed to grow slowly and therefor, the perfection he sought might not be something they could implement immediately.

He would need to find a base that would get them there over time. Back to the research!

Cairbre walked in about then and raised an eyebrow at the scene before them. He was just in time to see Gria smash Endarra over the head with an enlarged club, though she herself remained diminutive in stature.

He gasped then chuckled. "Don't let Endarra see this!" Another chuckle escaped him as he imagined the reality of the scene. It reminded him of the ancient human comedies played for children on what was called a *television.*

"So, I was wondering if you would like to join us for a foray into Kyra?" He glanced at Logori.

"You have been shut in so long people are starting to wonder if you are ok."

Surprise flashed across Logori's countenance as he was surprised yet again. This time at the thought that anyone *cared* about whether or not he did anything.

"Uh, yeah. Sure." He began closing his books and instructed Inlivia to save, then the two headed out.

"Where exactly are we going and what are we hoping to find?" Logori couldn't think of what might be out there when it had taken a near act of God to make this moon habitable.

"We heard some story about Octopi living on this moon." He caught the look on Logori's face. "We were never told the moon was uninhabited. Just that it would not be habitable for our own lifeforms without the energy boost. We assumed nothing was here."

Logori was a bit stunned by this revelation, but it quickly wore off as he realized the truth of Cairbre's explanation.

Thinking of his earlier conundrum regarding trade goods, things suddenly took another turn. This time he was excited about the idea that they may discover things unknown elsewhere.

His step became a bit more confident and purposeful as they suited up and grabbed the helmets off the wall near the airlock.

Gria flew by in a cute little suit of her own and an air bubble around her head. She was going to be their protection in the event they encountered that or another lifeform.

She smiled seductively then blew them a kiss as she zipped through the wall of the airlock!

Logori shook his head, sure he would never become used to that little minx!

Cairbre laughed. "She sure is a funny little thing!"

Stepping out of the airlock they nearly ran into a full human sized version of Gria in super seductive clothing. "Hello boys heard what you said in there, Cairbre. Think I'm still *a funny little thing*?"

She walked toward Logori, eyes on Cairbre, and ran her hands around Logori's chest and back as she circled him, moving her hips suggestively and licking her pouty lips.

Logori choked and Cairbre sucked in a breath speculatively then roared with laughter. This was a very unwise move on his part as he quickly discovered.

Holding his head in an opening in the ocean's crust, so close to outer space, she said sweetly, "Is this size more to your liking, Cairbre?"

He looked down and realized she must still have her feet on the ocean's floor. She was ginormous!

"No thank you, ma'am." At which she shook him like a rag doll. Glaring fiercely into his eyes.

He tried again, "I mean, no thank you, Gria. You made your point. Sorry." Relenting, she brought them back to Logori and let go of a visibly chastised Cairbre.

Damn, they were going to have to be careful of this one. She could make her own slaves out them, he thought as they followed her to the waiting group.

"Not interested. Have Brownies for that." She nonchalantly hurled back over her shoulder.

"Oh crap! She can listen to our thoughts!" He looked miserably at Logori. Logori just trudged along beside him wondering what he had gotten himself into today. Better not to think at all. He shrugged at Cairbre. "Maybe we should just think about the octopi?"

Cairbre nodded and tried to regain his composure as they walked up to the waiting group, realizing they had witnessed the entire event and were in varying stages of shock.

None of them had ever been around the Fairies long enough to realize the special powers they had. They mumbled their greetings and headed out at a brisk pace. Secretly hoping Gria wouldn't pick on one of them, too.

It took some serious travelling before they finally arrived at their destination. Looking everywhere, they finally found the area Gria had subdued the Octopi. The Sandy bottom was levelled and swept clean making it stand out in the surrounding ridges littered with rock.

They saw faint markings there, where the Octopi made their way back to wherever home was.

Following this trail, they came to a drop off into a trench. It looked to have no bottom, though they knew it was there somewhere.

"Hey, Gria. Could you do that thing you did earlier and check out the depth of this thing?" Doon was along as he wanted to watch for any signs of mining opportunities. This trench could well be their best chance.

Gria obliged. "About 40 ship lengths deep." Fairies were known for measuring according to whatever was around they could relate to. They detested math.

Pretty deep. They would need to wear better suits for mining there but maybe they wouldn't have to go so far down.

"Thanks, Gria." Doon smiled at her, eliciting one of her famous blown kisses and fluttering eyelashes. "Could you maybe do one more thing?" He glanced at her.

"Name it." She felt particularly benevolent toward this one.

"Light the trench so we can see if any color shows?" He raised an eyebrow wondering if she would comply. One never knew with her.

"Sure." She waved a hand and the entire trench as far as they could see lit up. There *was* color!

Bright spots of brilliant beautiful color! Doon's eyes fairly danced with excitement. Wait till Endarra heard about this.

He was startled by the thoughtful curious look on Gria's face. She became smaller then large again. Twirling and holding still breathlessly.

By then she had everyone's attention. "I hear something. Someone is here but it isn't the Octopi."

Deep in the rock, Beirnan slumbered, in a dreamless state now. Unaware of the group only a short distance from him.

Gria's eyes lit on the fish carcass. Picking it up delicately with her now shrunken hand, she waved it in front of them. "Fen-Folk." But I can't see the one I am hearing. It is such a faint sound. Like a heartbeat from many ships away.

Gria frowned. Something was wrong and as mean as she could be, she hated the thought of any being truly in danger. It was one of the endearing things about her and there were not many of those.

"Does anyone know where the Fen-Folk are encamped?" She looked round the crowd.

Diarmond stepped forward, "I believe they would be about as far that direction as the depth of this trench." He pointed South. Then wondered if a claim to the trench could be staked by the Fen-Folk as one of their own was firmly ensconced there.

Gria nodded, "Wait here then. I will be back soon." She was streaking toward the Fen like a slip of light shooting through the dark water. It helped when she discovered the path of crystals.

They had just all settled down to wait before she was back with Brenin and one of his scouts, Cledwyn.

She took them to the tiny little carcass and explained the sound she was hearing. *Obviously, she kidnapped them with no explanation. Typical Gria behavior.*

As they realized what was happening, Brenin began to look around in alarm. His future son-in-law was missing. They had just discovered his absence before Gria grabbed them. He had believed Beirnan had gone early to study and to ask for equipment.

With an examination of the surrounding area, they determined there had been a massive slide. If Beirnan had been caught in it, he was good and buried somewhere.

"Well what are we going to do about this?" He looked at Gria, then Cairbre, who had been introduced as one of their leaders. "I can bring all the Fen here, but we need excavating equipment to do this safely."

Cairbre nodded, "We can go get the equipment. Diarmond, Hamarre, Conn. If you would come back and help I think we can have it here in two cycles. We will have to gather some more help and I am not sure how much of the cargo has been unpacked. We will bring what is available."

So much for keeping the Fen-Folk separated from their new civilization! But perhaps they could still contribute something of value and maybe even grow a bit toward something resembling civilized.

CHAPTER THIRTEEN

Endarra rolled over and flung an arm out. Time for an early morning romp. But she encountered only empty bed. Opening her sleepy eyes, she looked around for Doon, seeing a note on the bedside table.

So, they had gone on a trek without her. No biggie. She stretched and yawned then rose and headed for the washroom.

It was time for a complete inventory of their resources and she preferred to get a visual while going over reports.

Poking her head into Alis' open doorway, she grinned at the scantily clad girl fresh from the shower. "Come on princess, duty waits for and respects no one!" Alis glanced down at her friend and threw a pillow at her head.

"So where are we starting?"

Endarra looked up at the five-foot eleven Elf, "Storeroom one on this ship for starters."

"Well let's go then," Alis grinned as the serious leader, Endarra practically scampered to keep up with her, looking very put out!

Relenting, Alis slowed to a pace in keeping with Endarra's walking stride. She chuckled, feeling all was quite right with their new home.

"Where did Doon get off to? I would have thought you would have kidnapped him for the day." Endarra looked only slightly miffed. "Out investigating Kyra. Seems we may have some natives afoot."

"Hmm." Alis looked thoughtfully ahead as they rounded the corner and approached the door they were seeking. "Has anyone seen them?"

"Oh, yes." She nodded emphatically. "Octopi, of all things, and who knows what else," she added grimly, hitting the door sensor with the palm of her hand for emphasis. "Got one in a Muir-Gheilt enclosure aboard this very ship!"

Alis raised an eyebrow. Rarely had she seen Endarra so perturbed. "When will they return?"

Endarra shrugged, "Who knows. They are exploring. I just hope they are not in over their heads and if they haven't returned by evening we will have to search for *them*."

Endarra stepped through the doorway and the automatic lights flickered on with a low hum.

Alis followed, scanning the room, sensing something amiss. She reached out an arm to block Endarra as she hissed, "Brownies!" Elves thoroughly disliked rogue Brownies and a rare few Fairies dared keep them like Gria did.

Brownies were ever vengeful and mischievous creatures that could never be trusted. They possessed a modicum of power compared to the Elvish but it was enough to cause immense discomfort to those they chose to annoy.

She slowly backed out of the room, pushing Endarra ahead of her and hitting the sensor, she wove an Elven Rune in the air, locking the contents within.

Time to visit that impish Fairy.

The two looked at each other then and burst into laughter. *Of all things!* "Brownies!" Endarra choked out.

The two eventually located the brownies and Gria contained their activities to her rooms.

The adventures of the new arrivals were varied and numerous.

****

Aelwen skipped ahead a bit over two hundred years into the vids. This portion of her history studies was almost too fascinating to let go of. The magic folk of today held only a fraction of their former glory. They rarely showed what they retained of that. Well, except for Gria and a couple of the Elves.

But let go she must, there was so much to learn.

The labs on Titan splayed across the screen, bring Mekhyr into focus as he readied the last of the populace for Enceladus. Portraying him through the eyes and understanding of the videographer:

****

During this amazing time of growth and as the generations came and went, it happened on Titan! The right combinations for two DNA lines held steady. When the first year passed with no deterioration, the Ancients moved to transport the remainder of civilization from Titan to the dome cities on Enceladus.

The Empagosan pilots slated to transport those carrying the special genome packages were to retreat thereafter, to follow their race to Parani. Parani being a dimension in the twists and folds of space directly linked to the Heavens of the Creator, in what Earthers called the Milky Way.

Taking one ship home with a small crew, from and returning to, the Jukara Galaxy, as the fallen *blinked* out of this dimension into Parani as they passed by.

Empwyn watched him in the lab as he removed genomes from the two Empagosans on the right and implanted the sleeping, gene manipulated, Muir-Gheilt on the left.

She could tell that even he needed to rest.

Their race needed little sleep, however the stress and constant work level he had become enmeshed in, was taking its toll on him.

Mekhyr set the instrument aside and nodded wearily to the surgery supervisor. He was finally done with the tens of thousands of transplants.

Knowing they could not produce offspring hit them hard in the early days. Their non-corporeal spirit bodies were fine, as Angels, but they were not satisfied to wait for humans to grow and take over their place in Heaven.

They wished to be those who would rule others like themselves. In their opinion it was wrong to place such inferior beings over them. But to do so, they needed to bring the longevity gene back into play for a select number of the *human forms* they had been manipulating with their own dna.

These had no soul so could be used as they wished. Splicing, into their own genomes, a life extender. They opted to retain all their powers and their wings. Creating a meshed façade of angel and human.

Over the next 3,000,000 years they perfected this to the point that now their, more or less, physical bodies appeared to be nearly indestructible by natural means, though if harmed they were still capable of the final act of life. Death.

Then the change started. Some 900,000 years ago. Weakening them to the point of escalated deterioration. Cohesiveness within the cellular level was diminishing.

The only way to survive was to have offspring and cohabit their bodies. They would not be born with soul as they were an abomination to the One having parents who defied Him. So, they would not be displacing viable beings. As pure angels, they had always been able to take physical form, such as when they procreated the Nephilim but only for a short time as it was severely draining. This was accomplished in a lab so did not interfere with other sentient beings. Other than for a few harvested eggs that is.

However, to achieve their higher purpose, they must retain physical form. Surely the One would take pity on them and include them in the chosen few to rule all creation.

Empwyn was close to Mekhyr and she was aware of his dedication to preserving their race even to the point of giving up his life in exchange for the life of a dedicated scholar and then scientist of the highest order.

Even more than that, Mekhyr had chosen finally, to sacrifice his own place with them to monitor the other life forms they were transferring to Enceladus and to gather back the genome packages he was now implanting them with, to save the future for the Empagosan race, or Ancients as they began to be called.

These packages were genetically directed to pick up the reproductive ability for Empagosans.

"Mekhyr, have all the packages been delivered?" Empwyn was anxious to signal departure.

Mekhyr paused as he injected the last of them into the brain of his current patient. "Yes, One willing, I can reintroduce them to our species dna as these carriers are finished with their life cycles." He bowed to his liege slightly and turned back to the table. "Send me the coordinates as soon as you arrive."

"It will take a few centuries of ongoing incubating to bring viable dna to term for storage in cryonics."

About every two or three hundred years the dimensional rift to Parani re-occurred, allowing inter-dimensional travel for those beings attuned to it.

When the genomes reached them, they would be able to reproduce with the markers the genomes will pick up from their carriers. Not with each other, but rather with the cloned ones to be hidden by Mekhyr in his special lab on Enceladus.

"Our race will survive." Knowing his hidden meaning, Empwyn hesitated as she made ready to go.

"Mekhyr, the transplants will survive, too. We've given them every opportunity. As they grow old and die, you remove the implants. No harm done. Their offspring will have virtually no imprinting from our genes. We understand your level of caring for these species and that is why we have chosen you to do this. Remember, no more alterations and no sharing of information beyond their natural stage of growth. I hope this works, Mekhyr, for as you know there are those who would rather strip out their dna now and stitch it to ours and be done with this process. They may still decide to act. Take care. I advise you to return with the genomes to your place with us."

As Mekhyr nodded gratefully, Empwyn headed for the transporter that would take her to the ships amassed outside the stratosphere of the moon.

True to form there was little emotion shared as the ships departed with their precious cargo. Empagosans toward the nearby dimensional rift to Parani and the rest, except for the Titans, to Enceladus.

Mekhyr drew a deep breath as his patients were wheeled out to his ship and he followed the Titans on board. He would spend the next one hundred years playing creator with the Muir-Gheilt in space before taking them to Enceladus.

The pilots who had carried the others to Enceladus would follow the other Empagosans in one of the empty ships after stowing the rest on the bottom of Kyra, Enceladus' ocean, and helping to move everyone to the domes.

All of the species were created to withstand complete immersion in Kyra should the domes fail. There would even be small islands adaptable for habitation for pure air breathers.

Mekhyr knew the combinations well:

> *Rhychdir a Titan and Eirlys an Ancient Empagosan were mated. Aelwen belonged to this matriarchal reigning class of Titan and Empagosan blood with the addition of Muir-Gheilt DNA.*

> *Another mating was handled similarly. Rhyawdd a Muir-Gheilt and Eneuawg a Titan were predecessors of Tristan. This ruling class was given the addition of Empagosan DNA.*

This line was made for water though they retain the ability to change to air breather.
These are called Eidan.

The reasoning for this was, if the domes failed, one ruling class would survive and complete chaos would not reign.

These strange combinations created certain differences in them when it came to childbearing.

Males from Aelwen's line can simply enter and return from the water at will.
They are called Elaran.

Therefore, when their maben are ready for birth, the males of Aelwen's line enter
the ocean and their legs which are permanently imbued with a thin and nearly
invisible layer on the inner portion become gummy and seal their legs together.

Their bodies then protect the process with a thin layer of skin effectively turning
their legs into tails with feet that form a fin like structure allowing them to swim
in the undulating movement peculiar to the Muir-Gheilt while allowing them the
freedom to function as human from the thighs up.

The undulating movement served a rarely thought about purpose. Balance and staying upright was challenging to a Muir-Gheilt. Arms did not make very good stabilizers. This skin sheds after the six moons it takes the maban to develop legs and the ability to survive in air. At the same time, the seal between the male's legs returns to its original state.

The women of Aelwen's line carry their young to term in the air at which time their second phase maban are born into the ocean and they are tended by their fathers.

For two month cycles the males hold the maben in a pouch like that of a seahorse.

Thereafter the maben are tended in the ponds like the others until ready to return to the domes as air breathers.

The females and males of the other line, called Eid, are permanently imbued with the ability to make this same change upon simply entering the vast ocean that is Kyra.

Likewise, the reversal is automatic. Special chambers, built into the domes, allowed them to transition easily to air.

These differences caused the majority to feel the female line Aelwen belongs to, are better suited to ruling as they are more accessible. These females are frequently called Eryi.

In Eryi gills can be forced to function by pushing on the point directly behind and below the ears. This is not to be done lightly as it takes a surgical procedure to return the gills to inactive stage.

For this reason, the Eryi choose most frequently to use breathers that separate oxygen from the water when they foray into Kyra.

The alternative are air bubbles complete with air packs carried on their backs.

These are used when the need to communicate will be necessary as they have built in mics and speakers allowing for interaction with all those around them, including the Muir-Gheilt.

The regular populace were Titans or average workers. When they married outside their race, the offspring took on the attributes of the other bloodlines.

****

Aelwen left the museum Theatre still immersed in the history films. She wanted to refresh memories that could help her with the upcoming meeting, nearly one thousand years later.

CHAPTER FOURTEEN

"Enceladus caused instruments on board the unmanned probe to detect a thin layer of oxygenated ice crystals around the moon.

The discovery suggests there is oxygen being released from the icy satellites of the solar system's gas giants, Saturn and Jupiter.

Showing that highly charged particles split the water in the ice into hydrogen and oxygen.

It is believed that Enceladus harbors a liquid ocean below its icy surface. The same is thought to be true of Europa, Callisto and Ganymede which orbit Jupiter. All due to the friction of rocks in the fragmented core which creates warmth under the ice crusted surface.

Professor Remulus is among a group of scientists lobbying the World Space Agency to send a manned ship to explore Jupiter's icy moons - known as the Titan mission, stating "These are fascinating places to look for life."

Titan, Saturn's largest satellite is another potential source of life, ergo the mission name. Its nitrogen and methane atmosphere is reminiscent of early Earth, according to Professor Remulus as he said, "It may be an Earth waiting to happen as the outer Solar System warms up."

Interworld Nasa is developing a proposal to send a craft to the ocean that is Enceladus' surface below the ice mantle.

"Interworld News"

It didn't take long for Earthers to follow through on what to some constituted a threat to a way of life and to others meant an incredible interchange of ideas and technologies was about to take place. They hadn't arrived yet, but their launch date was only five of Enceladus' months away.

True, they were going to Titan, another moon to Saturn and the mother moon to the current Enceladans though not much time would pass before they discovered the truth.

Especially if they happened to be looking when a ship *jumped* in the vicinity. Earthers were peculiarly persistent in dredging up every detail they could find in the universe.

Like a vacuum, sucking up every shred of evidence, especially since their newly won freedom among the stars, thanks to the recently developed CWAM, *crystal wormhole anti-matter*, the energy propulsion system they finally discovered the key to by reverse engineering the latest star ship to crash in the Sahara Desert about twenty of their years ago.

Though what they could possibly want on the ruined moon of Titan was anyone's guess. Even if they weren't thinking it was just starting to grow towards habitable instead of reverting as it was.

Nothing remained but deadly gases and polluted water. Anything that still managed to live survived on corrupted DNA and was likely as deadly as the moon itself. Titan now registered nitrogen and methane instead of oxygen and hydrogen.

Maybe that would throw Earthers off and they would perhaps discover another galaxy to ransack.

There was one other thing that was still in evidence, just waiting for discovery. Dwellings, business buildings, books and belongings. Earth's Anthropologists would have a field day if they were able to move around on the moon. And *if* they were able to discover the caves everything was built into to avoid damage from the never stable environment of Titan.

The caves that spanned three hundred levels and more, riddled the subterranea of the moon. Holding much of the original technology in use now, on Enceladus.

It was not as easy to unmake everything and knowing the cycle must once again bring Titan to a habitable environment, the Empagosans decided to leave it for that time. By then Earthers would have come close to the same developments anyway.

Everyone else already enjoyed these things and more on their planets. The secrets were safe for now.

It had taken every ship at the disposal of the Empagosans to transport everyone off moon. They had no warning when the gases began to spray from the ground.

The first geyser hit in the middle of the largest cavern. The most heavily populated. They lost a quarter of their people in that one night.

The terror was vividly imprinted in the ensuing chaos planted forever in Mekhyr's mind.

Thank the One it began slowly. Slowly enough to load them into spaceships they had never seen before. Brought through the jumpers last minute in a herculean effort to save lives.

Though, honestly, the Ancients did it for very selfish reasons. Not to say they didn't *care* about the Titans, just that they didn't care as much about them as they did their own goals and survival.

This would be the only way to *heal* the Angel DNA. Reliant now on the ones they had created against the will of the One to change the will of the One.

A ship-full of the Empagosans stayed with them for a while to ensure the new Enceladans had sufficient life support systems.

Though Empagosans otherwise known as dark angels, fallen angels, or those who created the Nephilim bloodlines, didn't need to travel by ship, oceanic or otherwise, it was easier to travel as a group this way.

Aelwen shook her head to clear it of the vids of the past reflecting on which side she would support at the meeting tonight as she noted her reflection in one of the multitude of "portholes" looking into the depths of the ocean around them.

She knew from her studies that portholes referred to ships on Earth but those were apparently miniscule in comparison. These "portholes" being as tall as she and wide enough for three or four citizens to be seen from the Maben beds, were vastly different.

She was very nearly the image of her mother in her youth other than for the red hair which was definitely a legacy passed on by her father.

Rhun had been long reclaimed by Enceladus, having fallen victim to a terrible accident while repairing a small jump station.

Even now the smaller jump stations were iffy. Too often one did not re-materialize at the other end and the technicians would go into a frenzy to *find* the lost molecules.

They were successful ninety-nine percent of the time. Though Aelwen could swear that those who were retrieved in such a way were missing a cell or two, usually in the brain.

She did miss her Father sometimes when she needed to share without being judged, for Rhun had a particular knack for listening that helped one feel comfortable enough to work a problem out with some ease.

Sometimes she wondered if their matriarchal society was the best way when she thought of what her father had to contribute.

Quite frankly Aelwen knew she was not the only one to think this but it was frightening to think of the alternative when looking at the example which was Earth.

It might be possible in some make-believe world, to *share* leadership but everyone, even males, knew that men in power would ensure the eventual destruction of civilization. At least if there was no balance.

The problem was in determining the rules for the balance. If it leaned too far either way, life would be disrupted yet again.

Having studied Earth's history extensively, Aelwen was acutely aware of the diminished role of women in their societies in the past.

They were abused, neglected, killed, tortured and treated as things across many religions, societal systems, races and time-lines, not to mention *other* perversions.

This was of particular interest to her as women everywhere were just as capable as men and indeed, her own race showed they were fully able to rule without all the fractious wars and fights that men seemed to crave.

Besides, men were built brawnier for a reason. To serve and protect those with less strength. Brawn did *not* mean Brain!

To be sure, female rulers seemed to work in their society, but other planets managed when they had male rulers. Not with as much finesse but then again, she shrugged inwardly as she battled with herself over the pros and cons.

What if they allowed Earthers into their lives to trade and exchange information. What if the

Earther's ideologies and habits became part of Enceladus.

What if the men of Enceladus found strong encouragement to take charge of their moon.

Here was the true reason for the debate today. Here was the dangerous idea in the library of reasons for continuing the isolation from Earth that they had maintained for so many centuries. Here was the one thing she could not address directly.

She turned away and knew she really had to choose whether or not to allow this interaction. Considering the subject she had just been reflecting upon, it was no easy choice and would bring many changes to her people.

It could potentially bring enough upheaval to completely disrupt their way of life.

She was the daughter of the reigning socio-economic class leader so there was no way out of this. She had to decide if for no other reason than to help protect the ponds. Without which their races would die out.

If Earthers were allowed would they respect the ecosystem of their ocean? They sure hadn't on their own planet. At least until recently.

Would they understand the need for this fragile environment to remain exactly as it was? The maben breathed this environment. The Fen-Folk and Muir-Gheilt too. As did those genetically altered for pregnancy and surrogate second stage pregnancy.

Artificial light simulating solar illumination brought out the brilliant jewel tones of the coral reef protectively encircling the crystalline structure of the ponds which glowed themselves with a golden warmth.

Colors so intense they nearly sang with energy. Emeralds, blues, gold, amethyst, rose tones and burnt orange were some of the more subdued colors of Kyra, emanating from the crystals and they represented every hue of the Universe in shining glorious rays of light.

The beauty of Kyra was most visible in the numerous dimly lit tunnels which had many "nooks" built in for outings, reflection, meetings and the talks she had enjoyed with her father.

Outer lights were angled away from the tunnels. For the moment the tunnels hummed with excited chatter as the subject on everyone's minds was the Earthers and what would happen next.

Would they send an emissary to Earth to open the lines of communication or would they, once again, vote to remain unseen and unknown to the Earthers?

Or would they simply send a ship out to meet them when they arrived to see Titan? Of course, the latter step would depend on Mekhyr as none of them knew how to fly a ship. Well, other than Gwyndolyn and Aelwen.

Much of the vegetation of Kyra was grown in these lights and usually it was the Muir-Gheilt tending the plants though now and then an Eidan or Elaran during transition was seen harvesting, planting or otherwise tending to their main food supply when not tending to the maban.

Of course, Aelwen's ancestors were responsible for much of that insistent curiosity from Earthers with their frequent *jumps* to and from Earth and their experiments while they played Creator until the real Creator smacked them for it.

The Fallen were allowed full reign in the underworlds until they interfered with the One's plans.

In a time prior to the relocation and genetic engineering of current Enceladans, when their ancestors, the Empagosa, maneuvered through space with the ease that Aelwen now moved through water, their distant home was denied them and certain features in their DNA were *disturbed,* as punishment, facilitating the need for restructuring of their genetic makeup.

This was when the Empagosans realized, millions of years ago, they had meddled in the DNA of Earth's inhabitants once too often.

But not just earth. They had meddled on so many planets and in so many galaxies.

Their own ability to survive was suddenly limited. Instead of eternal life, they now had several hundred thousand years. In gaining this bit of insight they decided to remove much of their other experiments from Earth and elsewhere.

Losing immortality was bad enough but the Empagosans or Dark Angels were punished further by being banned from earth.

While they were intruding upon the basic building blocks of their people, the ancestors simply went a step further to ensure survival and growth in the only place available at the time.

Titan. At least that was the official story.

Aelwen was certain there was more to this story but would have to wait until her mother was close enough to life's end or until she turned over the role of ruler to her daughter.

Until then all secrets shared with Mekhyr would remain Gwyndolyn's alone.

Aelwen really needed to return to the maben beds soon. She missed the siren song of the Muir-Gheilt as they tended the wee ones and worked the sea gardens.

The closest thing she got to time off was to assist in the jewel-toned ponds.

Wearing a breather, when alone or glass bubble when she needed to be able to speak to others, she could take her breaks wrapped in the fronds of plants, swaying to the current, warm and peaceful.

Her dreams during these interludes were exotic, beautiful and full of excited exploration, though she always woke feeling as though she slept for three cycles.

It was refreshing, though could quickly become boring to one such as she who thrived on multi-tasking and training for her future place in society.

The one thing that drew her back was the song. There was no describing the thrill of it. The utter wildness and raw passion of the sounds emanating from the Muir-Gheilt. It was beautiful beyond words and deserved the awe it inspired.

CHAPTER FIFTEEN

Tristan fell into step with the lithe young woman as she sighed at the inevitability of the encroaching conflict and returned to the task at hand.

Despite standing a good head and a half above Aelwen he hardly had to slow his pace at all. The dark haired, violet eyed boy stood on the threshold of manhood and his bearing promised much in the year to come.

As the contender's son, many expected a connubial match between the two upon Tristan's completion of the latest training course he was participating in.

It was a slight irritation to Aelwen that there was a contender for her future position as ruler of Enceladus.

This made it difficult to decide whether remaining and sending an Emissary would better serve her purposes or if going would elevate her in the eyes of the populace. Should they decide to interact with Earth at all!

Maybe she could send Tristan. Her lips quirked to the side as she tried not to grin at the thought.

"What do you want?" irritated at the possessive attitude Tristan exhibited whenever he was in her presence, Aelwen glanced over, succeeding in producing a frown.

"Not a thing, was just going to the meeting and saw you heading the same way."

More likely he was waiting around a corner knowing she had to be coming from this direction! With an indifferent shrug Aelwen glared at him. "If you insist on walking with me then I expect you to be circumspect and keep your *feelings* out of this meeting. At least where I am concerned!" *That ought to make him think twice about glaring at every male that looked her way like he did at the last meeting.*

What a stubborn female Aelwen is. Tristan stopped and acted the part of a mortally wounded victim. 'I have no idea what you are talking about, but if you think I have done anything less than be gentle with you, please tell me how." Tristan pleaded.

Aelwen snorted derisively and kept walking as she returned to her former thoughts.

She wanted to be the Emissary to Earth knowing that she would experience many strange and new things. She had been trained her whole life to take charge of Enceladus at the time of her Mother's retirement.

This challenge was always handed down from mother to daughter nearly all the way back to the beginning of creation.

Aelwen's line was descended from Rhychdir and Eirlys. The *other* line *always* challenged the new ruler.

The scepter had actually been handed off twice soon after the split in the ruling bloodline but had returned to Aelwen's family thereafter and had remained so until now.

She was sure this was half the reason Tristan wanted to commit to her. He thought it might give him at least peripheral power and so it would but Aelwen did not believe he would ever be able to handle such a load gracefully.

Tristan had a lot of growing up to do and she wasn't inclined to wait. The twerp was like a pesky brother to her for all that they were only nine monthly cycles apart.

At 229 lunar cycles old, Aelwen was ready to take her place as an adult of Enceladus and she had already completed her training courses in the ponds as well as leadership training while Tristan was only just about to complete the general training.

As a man he would not be allowed leadership training even were she to commit to him, though the merge would stop this infernal challenge as the bloodline would meld into one again.

The other half of the reason Tristan wanted to mate with her was devious and would be devastating to the Eryi.

They could never produce offspring. The match would simply make it easier for the leadership to fall to the Eid.

Though she was not yet ready to give up her independence, she knew what she wanted when such a time were to arrive.

A man who would take charge of love and family while allowing her the room to rule without being possessive and clingy, she glanced sideways at the runt with a relenting bit of humor.

She'd heard rumors that such issues were exactly the same for the men on Earth. It amused her to wonder how the males of Enceladus would handle such power and control with all the freedom the moon wide ocean, Kyra, afforded the females of their species and the children who enjoyed even more latitude.

The lights in the city were dimmed as simulated twilight darkened all. It was never allowed to become completely black like topside was rumored to be at this time of the moon turn.

The cities of Enceladus were located on the floor of the ocean. They were encased in domes with passages leading to each with Rashidan as the hub. There were a handful of domes surrounding each hub, used for various things.

Living quarters swayed in the ocean's currents, above the cities. Like aquatic high-rises barely anchored, just enough to keep from hitting each other or breaking free.

This kept the inhabitants in the flow of hydrothermal heat. This energy source kept them alive and made for engineering creativity.

They used a form of hydro energy elevator to raise and lower disks in the many vertical tubes.

Aelwen lived much of her time in Rashidan though she held spaces in various other cities as she frequently found political reasons to visit each.

Here though she held an entire area to herself and used it to entertain politically important Emissaries from other planets and moons for there was a brisk trade with other worlders who treasured the jewel like coral and crystals from this moon as well as a variety of precious metals and minerals mined beneath the ocean.

The crystals of Kyra were rare and matched those Earthers used to fuel their newfound ability to worm-hop.

Everything in the cities was a dark gray but for the brilliant crystal decorations and the surrounding ocean which teemed with colorful life unseen by off-mooners. To them Enceladus was simply a rock covered with water and frozen at the surface.

 To them, Enceladus was probably only good for the water supply and any nutrients they could dredge out of the depths.

Earthers were also discussing how to introduce sea life from earth that is dangerous for Enceladans and Muir-Gheilt.

This was too dangerous to allow and was sparking talk of war among some of her people. The intent was to determine if life could indeed exist in Kyra.

The thought made her shudder as she thought of the destruction of their young and vulnerable pregnant females with those giant monsters from the seas of Earth lying in wait in their own Kyra.

The biggest secret was lying at the bottom where a whole moon full of people were about to pass judgment on Earthers without Earthers knowing they even existed.

The reason they were about to pass judgment was not because Earthers were foreign to them. Nor was it because they wanted to be left alone.

It was because their most precious secret was about to be exploited and potentially destroyed if they were not very careful.

Ceithin stood as Aelwen passed through the ornate doorway with its delicate crystal scroll work and the brilliant encrusted minerals flashing a spectrum of fiery hues against the larger emerald green crystals.

She inclined her head regally as she glanced at him and then his new mate. "Good day, Svana."

Svana moved nervously and looked askance at Ceithin, feeling overwhelmed by the unexpected recognition. He touched her hand comfortingly and she breathed deeply in relief.

This couple was unusual in that Svana was not from their moon but from a neighboring galaxy in what Earthers called the Milky Way, though Aelwen could not for the life of her understand the analogy as there was nothing milky about the Way. It was simply a pathway to the Heavens.

Svana was born a top sider on her planet which harbored a small settlement from Enceladus in its largest ocean, Shyra, which was where she and Ceithin met and pursued their courtship.

The least concern Aelwen harbored was that the males of her species not turn to off world top-siders in any great numbers as that would begin to destroy their way of life and weed out the female Enceladans as they were now.

She had noticed of late that several young males were watching the interaction between Svana and Ceithin intently. They were excited by the power such a union would afford them. She would have to steer them to another diversion directly.

"Nairia, how are you?"

Nairia shrugged and smiled wryly at Aelwen, her friend since they were maban in the same pool. "Watching another batch of maban, Aelwen."

Aelwen glanced at her friend's obviously extended belly. *Fertile one, Nairia.* "Don't your mates give you any breaks? Didn't the last batch just make it to second pool?"

Nairia, as many of the Eid did, followed the old school relying on multiple mates to keep the species going, though the majority of the denizens of Enceladus eschewed the concept of females taking multiple male mates as the One preferred that they remained faithful to only one according to Mekhyr. However old habits and beliefs died hard with some of the population. Centuries hard.

It made sense that as the females ruled and they always produced multiple offspring, there would then be more than one male to help feed, teach and protect their shared little ones as they emerged from the ponds, while their mate was occupied.

"Just yesterday actually." Nairia chuckled. "And no, never a break for the weary." She nonchalantly tugged at a string of seaweed that had twined itself into her long black tresses.

Nairia was actually present at this meeting only through the use of a special chamber of which there were several in the room.

The chamber contained a specially formed halter to allow for the physiological changes in the Eid mothers.

Special microphones filtered their words through the water they were breathing and the chambers looked like bubbles encroaching from outside the domes through underground tunnels.

Elar did not need the special accommodations as usually only one representative attended these meetings. Ceithin was it this time.

Tarian smirked as she sat next to Nairia, remembering her youth and the tiny army of maban she raised. Her oldest was raising her fourth batch now.

Tarian was relieved to be backup and adviser at this point in time. The smirk covered a bit of jealousy if the truth were known. It was difficult to grow old.

It was considered in bad taste to raise more than four sets of two maban. There was a limit to the size of the moon they inhabited after all.

Though they did sometimes migrate to other water worlds, none were quite like home and of course, one always hoped the younger ones would remain close enough to attend the culling ceremony at the end of life's cycle.

Rumor had it that the dark deep here, held life as well. Other than the wild tribe of merfolk. But rumors were myths and she dealt with fact. However, myth though it might be, nobody was too willing to extend their lives to that area of Kyra.

Aelwen sat at the right hand of her Mother, Gwyndolyn, bowing slightly as she passed her. Gwyndolyn smiled lovingly at her beautiful daughter, well pleased with her quiet assurance and empathic demeanor. Both were excellent traits for a ruler.

It wouldn't hurt for Aelwen to visit a completely foreign planet to gain insight into another way of life though.

She needed to learn to handle tough situations and though the One was actually in charge He still expected them to follow through with His will and sometimes that took a lot of inner strength.

Gwyndolyn pursed her full lips thoughtfully as her large amber eyes scanned the room, looking for one last face.

Owena was there in the back talking quietly with her youngest who sat in another bubble chamber and was about to burst by the looks of her belly.

"Today, Owena?" her voice carried and Owena looked up, face beaming as she nodded. "Yes." She rose to make her way to the Council table, looking every inch the proud Grand Mother.

Tarian snickered at Owena this time and Owena glared in her direction as she seated herself with a huff.

It turned out the choice tonight was not whether or not to become known to the Earthers but rather how to allow that to happen.

There were pros and cons to each option. Allow them to eventually discover Enceladans or make them aware on their terms.

The first would buy them more time to prepare for the inevitability of the connection and enable them to provide more cloaking of the ponds to preserve their secret.

The latter would stop the Earthers from initiating any actions that could prove disastrous to their moon and lives on it.

As Aelwen's mother brought the meeting to order, Aelwen's thoughts drifted to the latest news flashes from Interworld News regarding the previous discussions that Earthers intended to transplant those sea creatures to their world in an experiment with the goal of deducing whether or not the amount of oxygen they would need to extract from the ocean was possible to allow for life on platforms top side.

Time was up. The first Earther mother ship was spotted yesterday. Where had the last few months gone?

It hadn't helped that Earthers had also perfected worm hole travel and launched two months ahead of schedule. Shaking her head, Aelwen sighed. She really disliked surprises!

Aelwen listened to all the arguments with due diligence though she found it difficult to not fidget as Tarian waxed eloquent on the many ways the women of Enceladus could benefit from the exchange of beauty tips with the Earth women.

Having heard the women there prized sea products for their faces and other skin, she was determined to be the creator of the first business to provide those things.

Svana timidly presented the idea that children would have better opportunities which cost Aelwen an involuntary shudder.

The very idea was destructive, however Svana, having lived elsewhere had a mind open to all the possibilities she could never un-realize.

Thanking them both, Gwyndolyn looked askance at Owena who stood suddenly.

Owena glanced at her daughter and took a deep breath. "Perhaps we should really consider the possibility that the medical information we possess could be increased with the Earther input. I know that we know far more than the Earthers but look at what they find among the indigenous peoples of their own planet even as recently as last year when they finally discovered how to cure cancer!"

"Perhaps we can learn from ones we consider inferior to us as well?" Owena glanced at the people in the room quickly and turned to look steadily into the eyes of Gwyndolyn.

"You do make a good point with this, Owena." Gwyndolyn sighed. She, too was not thrilled with the other possibilities but she was a good leader and understood that there could be much they would give up if they did not allow this interaction to take place.

Aelwen stood next, took a deep quieting breath and used the peace speak she learned at her Mother's knee when communicating with the people they were leading.

They were not rulers as Earth knows rulers. They were more like guides to the races that trusted them and allowed them to handle the details of conflicts that arose now and then.

"I know it is difficult to think of giving up what appear to be positive influences on our civilization. I am not so sure however that they are not fraught with pitfalls that we know little about." Aelwen dared not state the obvious knowing that Ceithin would pass on the entire contents of the meeting to the men of Enceladus, both Mer and otherwise. It would not do to make them feel that they were being repressed when for all these centuries they never really questioned their role in society. At least they hadn't until Ceithin and Svana came into Kyra. *If they get too close or do anything that will impact our moon, we will choose the time and manner of contact. If they however don't spend enough time in the area to discover us, we will let them go on their ignorant way and count ourselves blessed.*"

Nairia pushed the speaker button in her bubble, "I agree with Aelwen. What do we really know of the results of such an alliance with people who spend most of their time in one battle or another. We would certainly be providing them with more than they could ever hope to give us and we already have indirectly interfered with their growth with our crashed ships. Well, at least the Empagosans have." She hit the off button and sat back to see what would happen next.

Aelwen smiled at Nairia and turned to face the others. A fierce buzzing of voices filled the room as friends talked over the pros and cons of the contact and overcame the conflicting barriers that were inherent in such gatherings where there were opposing forces.

CHAPTER SIXTEEN

Rianna lazily flipped over and let the current sway her gently next to the first pond. Her beautiful tail moved gracefully back and forth in a motion that kept her upright with almost no effort. Rianna was a true Muir-Gheilt unlike the women of Enceladus.

There were 14,909 Muir-Gheilt in Kyra. 9,978 were male and 1931 were juveniles. Of those 803 were yet babes.

They were incredibly beautiful in coloring and graceful movement. Every color of the sea was reflected in the scales of their tails and their hair was long and silky, floating in the water.

Hair color ranged from silvery white to black as it did with humans on earth as their DNA was created from a mix of fish and human as well as Empagosan many centuries past by the Ancients.

Rianna waited patiently for her relief to rotate to her position. Only two more ponds and she was free for the next month.

Her shift consisted of two days in each of the three ponds, protecting the maban while their mothers and fathers assisted.

In exchange for this service, Enceladans provided protection for their race and ensured the delicate balance of life in Kyra.

There was the occasional treat such as a concert or play available to the Muir-Gheilt through the placement of bubbles throughout the gathering places in the cities.

It was good to interact, and it afforded the Muir-Gheilt a chance to obtain an education which many times worked into a trade able to be performed in Kyra itself.

Of course, there were also the genius Muir-Gheilt who worked as advisers in a variety of fields.

The maban and Muir-Gheilt children were allowed all the freedom of Kyra as the maban achieved growth that allowed them to leave the third pond.

This freedom did not last long as the maban had begun the transition by then and only for about half a moon could they be in both air and water.

For them it was the equivalent of a vacation from all care and all adults as they took the time to thoroughly investigate their moon. At least in the portion they could see in.

The outer and darker area of Kyra was still inhabited by Fen-Folk as well as beautiful creatures such as modified seals and whales, simple celled organisms and an abundance of fish and shellfish. Then there were the original octopi apparently native to Kyra.

Now and then the fish ventured into the inhabited area and became someone's dinner. The rest visited now and then playfully interacting with the Muir-Gheilt to the amusement of those watching from the domes.

The ancestors created food stations that they erected at intervals in Kyra. It filtered nutrients into a medium that helped the plants they transplanted to grow thick and healthy.

There was only one true danger in Kyra. The outer areas were black with no light reaching through the thick ice of the surface. Everywhere else there was at least a faint light from the cities. It was enough.

If one were to go into the darkness though, it was easy to become disoriented and travel below the equator. If this happened, usually the only way an Enceladan could return was through the aid of a Muir-Gheilt or the Fen-Folk, who though they also were blind in such places, had an inner guidance system that allowed them to sense direction.

As this was prone to happen quite frequently the Enceladans taught their second stage maban to whistle the moment they realized they were not in the light.

Then they were to remain where they were. Sound carried quite far through the water so they would be easily found.

The lower end of Enceladus was a deadly place to go. Nobody returned. That is, only one, out of the hundreds of lost over the centuries had ever returned from the deep.

Rianna daydreamed about her month of free time. Gareth had been showing hints of a desire to court her and she was more than amenable to such an overture from the handsome and daring Muir-Gheilt man.

He was, after all, quite a catch! All the Muir-Gheilt girls were half in love with him. He exuded a rugged strength and a very strong pheromone that spoke of many young. She could see herself surrounded by playful little ones as she lovingly attended to their needs.

"Rianna!" She shook herself free of her reverie, realizing Thara was here to replace her.

"Sorry, Thara. Guess I was getting a bit bored and slipped into a dream." Rianna's full lips curved in a wry smile.

"No problem." Thara shook a lock of silvery hair out of her eyes, making a face and said, "I get bored here too. Good thing it's only a two day stretch.

First pond was uninteresting compared to the other two ponds as the maban here did nothing but float and sleep as they began their journey into Enceladans.

Usually the mothers came and went with little regularity as there was so little to do and one could only gaze adoringly for so long before looking ridiculous.

The Muir-Gheilt ponds on the other hand were much more exciting as Muir-Gheilt babies began life as miniature replicas of their parents and were avid learners from the moment they hit Kyra. In these ponds the Muir-Gheilt learned everything they needed to learn to survive in the ocean with absolute freedom.

There were only two stages here. One for new babies and one for young that progressed to half grown.

There were Muir-Gheilt who took over from there to train the half grown to adulthood with a trade of some kind. These ranged from creating and maintaining private elimination stations to teaching Enceladans or participating in their counsels.

Rianna's skills lay in training the young to create the infrastructure of their own cities in Kyra. These were replicas of the Enceladan cities but for the water that flowed through them.

There were even bubbles throughout for Enceladans but these were fitted with air locks and were dry.

"Well, see you later." Rianna flipped her tail putting herself into a roll and with a fluid undulation she shot forward toward the next glowing area which was second pond.

There the maban were capable of communication though elementary in nature. They were rather cute which made up for the boredom she had just endured.

A shadow slipped up behind her suddenly and she gasped as strong arms surrounded her waist. She twisted around in the arms and was face to face with a smirking Gareth. Too sure of himself she thought reaching up to smack him on the chest with a small fist. Rianna scowled at Gareth, "What makes you think you can be this familiar with me, fish man?"

A satisfactory matching scowl hit his face to replace the smirk. "Come on Rianna. You said I could court you. Are you going to play hard to get now? Isn't that a little late?"

She smacked him again and he reluctantly loosened his grip enough for Rianna to squirm out of his arms. "Yes, you can court me. No, you cannot treat me as though we are already mated!" She turned, ignoring him as she pushed off for the pond again.

Gareth grabbed her tail and spun her around playfully mocking her. "I think I can be a little bit familiar with one I am courting, fish wife."

"You wish!" Rianna took off with a vicious tail flip, sending Gareth head over heels in her wake. She chuckled. That would teach him.

"Meet me out by the ship in five days?" Gareth laughed with delight at his intended's playfulness.

Rianna sluiced through the water with power undulations. She stopped briefly to grin and blow him a kiss. That was answer enough.

The *ship* was one of nearly an entire intergalactic fleet sunk by the ancients. It was rumored that they were still capable of space travel and were kept ensuring escape if anything happened to destroy Enceladus, too.

The one Gareth referred to emitted light due to the habitation of an ancient who kept tabs on the inhabitants of Kyra and was accessible through Aelwen's mother only. Well, sometimes through Aelwen.

As the *leader* of Enceladus, Gwyndolyn had many responsibilities, one of which was the transmittal of continuously updated files on every citizen of Enceladus for the perusal of the ancients who were informed through Mekhyr.

Mekhyr shared only that the genetically engineered DNA of Titans was not quite as stable as the original DNA created by the One which meant that the biological makeup of every living being on Enceladus was a time bomb ticking toward physiological melt down.

These updates could provide an answer that would enable them to push that date forward.

So Gwyndolyn made a monthly pilgrimage to the ship via a portable bubble carried by two of the Muir-Gheilt and found that she rather enjoyed the visits as she was privy to artifacts and technology she would not have known existed otherwise.

Gwyndolyn had been off moon a handful of times to neighboring planets and moons and once even jumped all the way to a star system in the next galaxy but it seemed that the ancients had not shared their technology with anyone. At least not in any of those locations.

As the ship Mekhyr inhabited tended to heat the surrounding water and provide small rays of shimmering light in the vicinity, new lovers were inevitably drawn to it for short trysts cultural and spiritual protocol would not allow them within the confines of society within which they were always watched carefully prior to a structured acceptance ceremony with a mate.

Of course, everyone knew this happened but looked the other way knowing that as the codes of conduct were strictly enforced, they taught the young to be respectful of the societal laws enough to curb their instinctual appetite for interaction until it was time for a permanent mating.

It was important to allow them time to be open with each other however, and they were never really alone with the ancient monitoring the surrounding area.

As it was Mekhyr and the other Ancients that taught them the mores they lived by, they all relied on Mekhyr to inform Gwyndolyn of any untoward activity.

An added thrill enjoyed by the young adults was the occasional glimpse of the *Dark Angel* as the Ancient was called.

Now and then, through tiny slit portholes, one could see into the interior of the massive dark ship. Rarely, someone would catch him moving about.

Curiosity was obsessive as they tried to discover what exactly the *Dark Angel* did in there all this time. The truly lucky saw him turned away from them and were granted a glimpse of the fabled wings.

As it turned out, Mekhyr was, at the moment, putzing around the galley, preparing a simple meal.

He was tall and darkly handsome, hair jet black and with enormous black eyes.

Enceladans had come to see him as some sort of Spiritual Guide when nothing could be further from the truth.

Although he *did* inform them of the Creator and the general direction He was located and he *did* pass on to them the teachings the One had given their ancestors, Mekhyr was in no way a Spiritual Advisor, having very little of the thing called emotion.

His race was so Ancient that not one of the Empagosans remembered hearing of their origins. Only that their home lay outside the known Universe. They located Parani in a twisted fold of time space and believed it to lead to the Heavens of the Creator.

They were there now waiting for Mekhyr and the DNA bank. Being the Dark Angels, the Ancients mistakenly created the Men of Renown, the giants of old but they leaned toward delving into the manipulation of creation to serve their own ends. The evil ones were their first attempt to create in the realm of the One, or God as many on Earth knew Him as.

They were of the faction that jealously watched as the beings created by the One scraped their way through life, stumbling and mangling everything.

To know that these inferior beings would inherit the Heavens and rule over them was too much to bear and if it took assimilation to be a part of that glorious reward, well then, they would certainly assimilate.

Problem was, He did not give them that option so they were taking it. If they could achieve the goal of genome impression of the required genes by the methods Mekhyr used, their vision was attainable.

If not, they were as good as lost for they were away too long, with infinity gone, and their stolen DNA, that which had allowed them corporeal form for all these eons, was coming to an end.

Mekhyr was to also teach the leaders how to run the ships and to give them history as well as cultural details.

He had spent the last thousand years observing their growth and interactions through mini camera units set high in the domes of the cities. They focused on both Kyra and populace. This information was relayed to Parani.

He had one other function which he really did not care for. Once a month he traveled into the deep to take readings from the sensitive instruments planted as far away as even he dared to go.

He didn't even like to think about his "real" reason for avoiding the deep. The multitude of blowholes which spontaneously spewed water from Kyra.

This was achieved through the use of a small ship with manipulated *arms*. He traveled in the dark edges to get to the area he needed to be in before heading down and now and then a Muir-Gheilt or maban or even an Eidan or Elar during transition would see a portion of the small ship which could actually fly if it left Enceladus.

Mekhyr was just not anxious to give it a test run. He called it simply the small craft or craft.

When the ship was glimpsed, it fed the fear of monsters in the deep with its shadowy waving arms.

This suspicion was not corrected as now and then someone who entered the deep never returned and it served to keep the majority out of the deep through fear.

The truth was, there were jets of water and ice spraying into space from the south polar region.

These appear as a small white blur below the dark pole, down and to the right of the illuminated part of the surface of Enceladus.

The Enceladans that never returned met their end spewed from Kyra into space with the ice and water.

However, near Rashidan, Rianna felt warmer in this region of Kyra, near the ships. Most of the hot springs of Kyra surfaced here.

It wasn't really all that comfortable but it seemed that passions ran concurrently to the water temperature so maybe it was worth the discomfort after all.

She chuckled thinking of the last time she met Gareth in these waters. Looking quickly around,

Rianna slipped around the ship so she could frighten Gareth when he arrived.

She ducked below the little windows to avoid detection from within and suspecting nothing, she backed into the small ship as it left its dock, arms floating in the water.

As one of the arms brushed against her back, Rianna's halter became snagged and as the sudden fright caused her to black out, she heard Gareth's voice from so far away.

She struggled to call out not realizing her voice was no more than a weak whisper as her body went limp and she was dragged along in the wake of the monster.

Gareth lounged against the hull of the ship watching for Rianna. He had been waiting for so long he began to worry that maybe she wouldn't come after all.

Doubt assailed him as he thought of all the reasons she might not. What a fool he was to think that she felt the same way. The last time they met she had ditched him.

She never let him hold on to her for long and kept a certain distance between them. How ridiculous he felt as he finally pushed off for home. Barely holding to his hopes, Gareth turned over the events of last night in his mind.

Tail twitching in irritation, he became angrier by the minute, feeling humiliated at being stood up. Well, see if he asked her to do anything again. It was over.

There were plenty of females who tossed their hair and giggled when he swam by. Rianna thought too highly of herself, perhaps trying to emulate the attitudes of female Enceladans.

Humph. He snorted and shoved off in search of breakfast. Gareth viewed partial and full air breathers as another group entirely. He was always perturbed by the races intermixing but shrugged it off as something he could do nothing about.

Though Rianna acting like them was another matter.

By evening, however, seeing no signs of Rianna, Gareth began to realize that maybe there was a serious problem. After an agitated night, Gareth decided that if she was not in her nesting area, he would go to see Gwyndolyn.

Stomach roiling at the thought that he had been angry and wasted time when Rianna could be in danger, he sped toward the ponds which is where Rianna lived.

The Muir-Gheilt didn't have homes as those in the bubbles had. Their lives were much freer and they often changed nesting spaces. Other than for the Muir-Gheilt dome cities that served to allow interaction with air breathers on their terms.

They accumulated odds and ends like beautiful crystals and corals. They even spun incredible structures out of sea minerals to surround their areas but when they became bored it was easy to walk away and find another nesting area and the process would begin again.

Either someone else would move into the area they just vacated or Kyra would reclaim the minerals and return the site to its original pristine condition.

CHAPTER SEVENTEEN

Mekhyr guided the ship along the usual path far into the deep dark waters of Kyra. He waited until he was far enough in that lights would not reach back to the larger ship before flipping the overhead lever which not only turned on the outer lights but also the inner, allowing him to finally turn on the auto pilot so he could move about.

The trip would take several hours so he settled back into his chair with a good book and steaming cup of tea.

Somewhere along the way, the arm holding Rianna turned enough to dislodge the precious burden it had carried so far and Rianna floated softly to the sea bed unaware of the danger she was now in.

Mekhyr finally finished his errands and headed back to the mother ship making good headway on the circular trip.

As he recorded his day, he sleepily yawned and prepared to shut down the lights, to approach the last two hours in darkness, when he suddenly caught sight of movement on the ocean floor.

Rianna moaned and turned over feeling pain in her back where she could not reach though when she tried her hand came away feeling sticky.

With what, she could not see but it mattered little as she lost consciousness yet again with the understanding that somehow, she had been dumped in the deep dark and there was nobody to help her. Just before everything went black, Rianna felt the force of Kyra's rejection as she flew up and out into equally black space.

When Mekhyr finally reached her, he knew they had been observed by the earthers.

No! Oh please, no... Rianna moaned in pain, wakening, as the metal arm grabbed her around the waist.

Why couldn't she get loose? What had happened? Was anything broken?

Myriad questions filled with fear made her head feel woozy and dizzy, threatening to take her over the brink of sanity as she struggled to be free.

Heart beating in her throat, Rianna's second instinct was to make sure she did not break free of the only contact she had with a tangible unknown.

As opposed to freefall in the darkness with no point of reference.

Mekhyr could not reverse direction fast enough to prevent their exit into space.

The next few moments removed the only choice she could make and Rianna began to gasp as water became thin and she was pulled back into Kyra.

"Gareth", the scream ripped from her throat and she saw the glory of space briefly before succumbing to the inner blackness of her mind.

"Did you see that?" Jeffrey gasped in shock. He watched the tiny ship as it launched from the blowhole on Enceladus and shook his head sharply, trying to dispel the other image. The one of a, no. This kind of thought led to madness.

Jeff glanced at his buddy, Aaron. Wanting to ask if he saw the same thing and realizing from the look of awe on Aaron's face that there was no need to ask. He had seen her. The half fish half human. The Mermaid!

Aaron lashed out, grabbing at Jeffrey's arm in an attempt to find reality. "You don't happen to see, uhm, anything odd about this do you?"

He wasn't about to be the first to have to visit the mental ward of the infirmary. No way was that vision real, but she wasn't going away, was she? And then she did.

Jeffrey sat back and rubbed his eyes. When he opened them again the ship and the, thing had vanished. Hallucination. That's what it had been. Group hallucination. He'd read about the phenomenon.

Aaron, however, was still staring wide eyed at the screen. Stuttering slightly, he tried speech. "Wh what w was that, Jeff? That woman fish thing, that wasn't real was it? I saw a tiny space ship and the thing and then they seemed to just get sucked into the blowhole."

"Oh, crap!" Jeffrey reached for the mic controls. "Life! There's life out here!"

Silence was his reward and seconds later, "Repeat please. "

"I said, Life. And you are not going to believe what kind!"

***

Mekhyr didn't have to think about his reaction as he simultaneously saw Rianna and the Earther ship. The only thing he could do was save his charge from asphyxiation. Ensuring security would just have to come later.

He returned to his starting point in record time. Donning a suit, he left the safety of his ship and extricated Rianna from the metal arm holding her.

As she was limp and he feared for her wellbeing, Mekhyr broke protocol.

First fitting a water helmet over her head, he towed her to the airlock of his home ship, he lifted her and carried her to a long unused water room.

These rooms were special built to transport the water creatures to Enceladus in the first place.

As he anxiously patted her arm, Mekhyr rapidly ran through the assorted options available to him. Kill them, no, Reason with them, no, Kidnap them. Of course. As soon as Rianna was safe. He could keep them off the ship they were in and well, he would figure the rest out later. There always a mind wipe, hmm.

Due to a slip of a half human/half fish, his own race stood squarely in the mouth of destruction.

He had to find a way to keep anyone from further contact for at least a year. He was so close to harvesting the last of the genome packages.

Most of the cryonic tubes were filled with precious life. He could not risk Enceladus being overrun by the scourge of Earth.

He had seen their takeovers. Their motives were good, but their reasoning was barely evolved past the animal stage.

Mekhyr nodded encouragingly in her direction and hurried off to his small ship.

First things first. Talking rapidly into the mic, Mekhyr convinced a somewhat reluctant Gwyndolyn to leave all in Aelwen's hands to sit with Rianna until he could return with his captives.

Gwyndolyn entered as Mekhyr's craft was leaving. "She has had a bad shock. Help her be calm, will you? We cannot let her go back with tales of this. I need to leave briefly and will be back before the next cycle. Will you stay here under some pretense with Rianna until I return?" Gwyndolyn replied, "Affirmative", into the mic, knowing she would get the story soon one way or another.

Unwilling to share the new events with the population just yet, Aelwen had given an even more reluctant promise to her Mother. She would wait until she had more information and could formulate a plan of action.

Aelwen gazed anxiously toward the ships. Well, the meeting this morning was probably meaningless.

They may no longer have a choice. Drawn into the whirl of discovery by fate, One help them!

The sigh came unbidden from somewhere deep within her, shocking her into the realization that she was more worried that they would choose not to communicate than she was now that they had stepped over the brink of discovery.

She could not deny the excitement creeping slowly through her being. Fear there was aplenty but who knew what wonderful things might come of the interaction with Earthers.

Much about them was wrong. Wars, senseless destruction on an individual level, selfishness and greed were only the tip of that consensus. Then there were all the good things. The determination, love, ability to empathize, inventiveness and resourcefulness to name a few.

They were a fairly old race, like hers which, though genetically altered, could trace its bloodlines back to nearly the beginning of the Universe.

Because of this strong and stable foundation despite moves and that genetic alteration, Aelwen had a sense of continuity as did her people.

It came with a price. The never-ending battle to avoid complacency. Boredom. If a people were not growing they were stagnating and stagnation meant death.

They avoided this to some degree by allowing the few off worlders in by marriage. It helped to have the Merfolk and to move between water and air periodically. But even that got old quickly enough.

***

He wished it was his own but that was not yet set up for an automated maneuver such as he needed to make now. However, he had made a promise to Gwyndolyn to recover the spaceship discovered when rescuing Rianna.

Desperate to locate the ship he'd seen, Mekhyr made record time to the blowhole and wincing, launched himself through it.

His plan counted on coming up behind them undetected. For this purpose, he'd chosen a blowhole some distance from the one they would be watching.

He manipulated the mechanical arms into position to catch their center firmly and used hyperdrive in short, light bursts to push them toward the blowhole before they could react.

Jeff attempted to warn the mothership of the abduction only to find the communications channels jammed.

Going through, he had them at a disadvantage in the darkness until they turned on their lights. But by then he was already halfway home with them and they were not trying overly hard to break free. Curiosity no doubt. Their race had its issues but he had to admit they were courageous and persistent.

They obviously wanted to be taken to see the Muir-Gheilt. He would oblige them, ensuring their peaceful cooperation.

He nearly smiled at the thought but was too aware of how fast a circumstance could turn.

Jeff sat open mouthed, staring through the "window" at the blackness as it began to brighten and recede, leaving in its wake a myriad colored undersea castle. Dear God in Heaven, he spoke reverently. A fantasyland, a fairy tale, a damned incredible discovery, if you could call being kidnapped a discovery!

Aaron was similarly, in awe. What is this? They had obviously been taken but were they prisoners? Guests? Whatever they were, it was shocked half to death.

Not that long ago, just knowing other planets had to be populated was enough to solicit this type of response. Now it was known that there were many races and few truly resembled the shape they had but never had he seen the fabled Mermaid.

But, if they were here how could they be a myth on Earth? He watched as several of the same emerged from the water castle, obviously trysting. He rubbed at the blur in his eyes completely unaware that he was tearing up at the sheer magnitude of their discovery. He didn't care who dragged them through the experience. Shrugging off the emotional response his next thought was more in keeping with his nature. More in keeping with the reason he was in space to begin with. Scientific exploration of places, things and lifeforms. He was already trying to think of a way to return with a sample. It would have to be an embryo. They would have to smuggle it directly into the cryonics lab onboard.

"Jeff, look at that!" Aaron was near to exploding as he pointed at several bubbles in the water. Three held Fairies and one held what could only be an Elf. All three looked ancient to his eyes. And beyond understanding. For once Aaron was speechless.

Jeff was impressed. He couldn't remember the last time Aaron couldn't speak.

He used to drive Jeff up a wall with the constant noise. Jeff had learned to tune him out so that recently he hardly noticed but when it stopped, he noticed all right.

Turning to look at whatever Aaron was viewing, Jeffrey sat down hard in his seat. "No way." He couldn't think of anything else to say. "No way," he repeated.

"Yes wwway," stuttered Aaron, finally coming out of his shock.

"What did we eat this morning? This cannot be real." he stated with utter conviction. It had to be bad food packs. They were seriously hallucinating. He rubbed his eyes and shook his head then peeked through one barely open lid. They were still there.

Jeffrey was equally determined to fight his way out of the fantasy world he thought they were in. Did Aaron see what had grabbed their huge ship? A tiny ship with mechanical arms of all things. Then he saw a gigantic ship that made his seem like a babe. This changed his demeanor rather quickly as he realized they were out machined.

Beyond the ship were incredibly engineered multi-level domes separating the water from regular looking people, from this distance anyway. The two looked at each other with relief. A bit of sanity might be coming their way.

There appeared to be glass hallways or tunnels running along the edge of the domes and they seemed to link from dome to dome.

Just this side of the domes were what looked like lit underwater basins and no matter how hard he tried he couldn't see anything or anyone else. It was a strain to see what he had.

Turning back to the ship, he noticed a few dim lights shining through the water, like rays from the sun. Jeff felt a touch of nostalgia.

He did miss home even though this was the find of the millennium. He'd kept the camera on since first visual as they waited for the scene to recur.

All of this was being recorded. Then he realized the light he'd seen from the domes and basins had faded to nothing. The only light now came from the ships.

They came to a halt, abruptly, throwing him back into his seat then he pitched forward onto his face.

Rubbing his sore nose, feeling very undignified, Jeffrey rose to his feet and headed for the airlock.

He was ready to abandon ship for a while. Aaron was only a step behind.

Putting on suits took a few minutes then they were out, face to face with their discoveries. For a brief moment nobody moved then, from behind, they were both grabbed and their arms restrained.

CHAPTER EIGHTEEN

Jeffrey Hanson
Mission Biologist & Ship's Captain

I woke in a room with curved walls. They must have brought us to the big ship. I struggled to remember anything beyond leaving the airlock. It came in tattered images.

We were attacked and a brief skirmish ensued, resulting in blackness. Then this.

I rubbed the back of my neck, easing the pain somewhat while taking in the sparse furnishings. A floating chair complete with a swinging arm table.

Floating balls of light and what looked like a horizontal cocoon but must be a bed. One wall was imaged with one scene after another.

A low hum reminded me of engines and fans. It was darn cold in here for all that. Moving around to keep warm, I examined the walls for any evidence of a door or portal. Rewarded finally with a hairline fracture in the wall with all the scenery.

Feeling along the edge of the line, I searched for anything resembling a latch when suddenly the door swung out and I began to fall forward.

An arm swung in to catch me and I found myself face to face with a being so far removed from my ability to accept that all I could do was choke out gasping sounds in an effort to voice my shock.

A male looking countenance gazed warily at me above the collar of a white robe. His face was beyond beautiful, it was darkly noble.

But the crux of the matter refused to blink away when he turned to walk into the next room, leaving me in the hands of his friends. His entire form was covered in folded wings. Beautiful, graceful, dark angelic wings.

I staggered and reached for anything solid. Anything to help me stabilize the racing thoughts provoked by his appearance.

"Who who who," I sounded like a freaking owl! Swallowing hard, I tried again. "Who is that?" Even though it still sounded like little more than a croaked whisper, the woman observing me answered simply, "Mekhyr."

Looking askance at her remark, she relented and explained briefly. "Mekhyr is an Ancient here to help us." She shrugged away my still questioning look and said, "Bring him to the lab." Grabbing me on both sides, I realized there were two males in this group and they were not fooling around.

"Where is Aaron," I raised my voice enough for the woman to hear me as she stepped through the next opening. She didn't even bother to turn as she answered, "In the lab".

As they pushed me through the next room to the lab, I glanced around, looking frantically for anything that would allow for escape from this crazy place with merfolk, angels, elves and fairies! Surely I was in lockdown somewhere safe, having a friendly little crazy hallucination!

CHAPTER NINETEEN

Aaron Goldberg
First Mate & Ship Engineer

Dang! What had caused the back of my head to feel like a truck had run over it? Reaching gingerly to feel for the damage, I winced and tried to sit up.

It appeared I had been dumped into what looked like a cocoon. Thinking about the sci fi horror films I had seen as a kid, I couldn't bail out fast enough!

Ouch, my head started pounding as I hit the floor on all fours, my legs not yet ready to take the weight of my body.

Crawling to the cocoon I grab the edge and pull myself up just as a portion of the wall to my right swings open.

No, no no no, I want to go back to sleep now. I cannot cope with the vision staring me in the face! An Angel? A Demon? An illusion?

"Need more time," I managed to plead. More time, as the beautiful dark being reached out and I lifted my hand to touch his glowing black wing.

Then I woke on a hard surface in what appeared to be a rather high-tech lab. Taking a moment to get my bearings, I swung my legs over the edge and sat up feeling a bit on the woozy side.

A few minutes later, I heard sounds indicating the approach of several people.

Thank God! Jeff appeared unhurt but definitely restrained. OK we need to figure out how to get out of this but maybe first it would be good to listen to what these people or whatever have to say.

***

Mekhyr searched for blankets stored in the warmer and handed one to each of the men, motioning to Jeff to have a seat next to Aaron.

Mumbling a bit to himself he then left the room and came back in short order with two cups full of a steaming liquid that smelled faintly like booze.

Handing these to them also, he asked if they were hurt anywhere, getting hardy winces from both as they reached for the back of their heads.

Mekhyr looked accusingly at Fahro and Jente who both sheepishly grinned back at him.

Fahro offering, "Sorry, we haven't ever had to do that before and guess it was too hard."

Jeff lashed back, "It wasn't necessary at all, moron! We would happily follow you in here." His glare promised he was not done with them.

Turning his attention to Mekhyr, Jeff asked, "What is this stuff," motioning his chin toward the cup in his hand.

"You would call it a calming tea," Mekhyr responded. "Drink. It is just what you need after being knocked out."

"We apologize for the way you were greeted but you pose a fundamental problem for us. Unfortunately, some of us over reacted," he scowled at the two guards. "Why don't you two wait in the other room."

When Jente started and began to voice his concerns about this arrangement, Mekhyr spoke sharply, "Now!" Relenting slightly, he said, "I will call you if you are needed."

Jeff sipped at the tea and gave a nod of approval so Aaron tried it as well, grinning as he identified the brew. Hot spiced rum!

Jeff saw Aaron begin to tilt as Mekhyr caught him and watched as he was lowered until he lay on his side before he realized he was going out and tried to stand. Mekhyr caught him as he began to slide into oblivion. The sob drugged us was his last coherent thought.

Gwyndolyn and Mekhyr relocated the two men to an outer locker. One of many on the ship's perimeter. Locking access, it effectively became their prison until he could decide what to do with them.

The two walked back to his quarters quietly lost in their own thoughts about this unexpected turn of events.

"We could…."

Mekhyr waved her thoughts back. "No, Gwyndolyn, we will not consign them to the deep. We are not murderers! Think of something else and we will talk."

She glared at him then relented. He was right. She couldn't live with herself if she caused their deaths. But it would be much nicer if the Ancient one couldn't read her thoughts. She laughed suddenly as he glared back!

She knew he thoroughly disliked her referring to him as ancient. It was obvious how he felt about her and though she reveled in the small power she held over the dark angel who wielded power beyond her ken, at times like this it was almost fun to poke at his sensitivity.

He glared again and she chuckled, turning away as she tried to hide her grin.

Mekhyr rued the day he let her go to Rhun. She challenged him and tormented him. Gwyndolyn was the real reason he chose to stay.

He could have left anyone else from the lab and they would have done the transfers credibly well.

He couldn't stand the thought of never seeing her again. It was painful knowing her love belonged to Rhun and even more painful to watch her give birth to their child, knowing he could never have given her that joy.

But ultimately it was him she turned to now and he began to hope. Just a slim ray but for now it was enough.

She knew this also and was content to do nothing, watching the scene unfold as though she were watching from a distance, for her heart was still bound to the man she loved with every fiber of her being, though she would never be by his side again.

She loved him through the memories they had shared and through their wondrous daughter. And through the life they helped build here in this watery place.

"What are we going to do about these two?" Gwyndolyn looked at Mekhyr, noting his unusually agitated state. Was there a contingency plan for Earthers showing up in Kyra? They *could* keep them hostage, she blurted as Mekhyr raised a hand in silent plea for silence. "Let me think!" Mekhyr snorted. Why did females here *always* have to talk so much in a crisis.

The entrance portal opened revealing her daughter coming through the narrow passageway. "Aelwen?" Whispering in her mind the question, "Why are you here? You know you are not allowed." Aelwen answered with a look that said it all. Danger was at their doorstep. They used mind-speak genetically reserved for those rulers of their line and imparted by Mekhyr at birth.

"What is it?" Gwyndolyn's heart caught in a vise, as she imagined the worst.

Aelwen shook her head, "Mother, you need to see Earther news, as she crossed the mostly empty grey room to the screen nestled among the dials and switches."

Mekhyr startled her, "Do Not Touch my things young woman!" She whirled to face him and backed away from the ferocious countenance before her.

"I wasn't going to do anything," She stuttered in self-defense then drew herself up and glared at him regally, hearing her Mother chuckle in the background as she watched her precocious daughter spar with the Ancient.

Mekhyr was secretly pleased to witness the inner resiliency of the next Ruler. He, however, wasn't about to let her know that. "I will thank you to keep your inquisitive fingers to yourself."

"These are delicate and irreplaceable." He scowled at her. She gazed at him, unconcerned and yawned as she dismissed the devastatingly beautiful dark winged Angel as if he were Tristan. She knew he could crush her with a thought. She felt empowered though, regardless and squelched the desire to throw a barb, knowing she would, one day, work closely with him and wanting to keep the peace.

"You might be interested in knowing Earthers are coming to locate these two. They do not know for sure where they are and are going to Titan first."

Gwendolyn looked at Mekhyr, "Did they have time to give any definitive information when you brought them in?"

Mekhyr reflected on the circumstances of the abduction, "No, I jammed their signals before they ever saw me and they neglected to say where they were exactly when they reported Rianna."

Aelwen, feeling bored with the situation at hand, unable to speak with the Earthers until they woke from the drug induced sleep, thanks to Mekhyr, said her goodbyes and left for home. She yawned again, this time for real and suddenly became aware that she had not slept for two cycles.

She had noticed the electrical charge in the room as she entered earlier and had no wish to interfere. It was something she puzzled out sometimes when alone. She knew her mother would never take another of their own to mate.

Everyone knew how deep the love between her parents had run. Nobody would be able to fill his place. But the Empagosan, on the other hand, she shrugged thinking, if he caused any small happiness in her mother, well she knew it would be emotional rather than physical anyway.

Gwyndolyn glanced at the Dark one as he thoughtfully threw the used blankets into the recycle tube.

He felt her question.

"We will do it. but it must be done carefully. You will have to fly the Earther ship and short jump to my ship." He looked apologetically at her as she sucked in an audible breath, knowing her husband had perished doing a similar short jump.

"I would go in your place", he paused and tried again, "If anything happens I will be able to retrieve you, but if it were myself, you may not succeed."

She knew the truth of this simple, honest statement and respected Mekhyr for his blunt consideration. Yes, she was afraid but more afraid of what Earthers could do to them in large numbers.

She didn't try to avoid the memories of their history and what they did to those they considered weaker than themselves.

"We will need a distraction." Mekhyr glanced appreciatively at the heart-stoppingly beautiful creature before him.

Gwyndolyn was one of their most satisfying accomplishments and if she had not married Rhun, he may very well have attempted a liaison regardless of the spiritual and physical implications. After all, how different was an actual relationship when compared to all the genetic manipulating they had done? But he shook the thoughts off now and marveled at her strength and determination.

"Now, go and rest, Gwyndolyn", he spoke softly this time, with a hint of the feeling he carried for her.

She nodded. It had been long since she slept and what she was to do would take all her concentration. She reached for her bubble.

He reminded her for the millionth time, "I could make it so you could breathe air or water." He hesitated hoping she would capitulate this time but as usual she refused with a small shake of her head and said, maybe another time.

He felt the loneliness as she entered the water.

CHAPTER TWENTY

The Fen-Folk were the most adventurous and hardy of the merfolk, being infused with shark DNA from Earth. They resembled more the Fen-Folk of earth lore and had serrated teeth. Normal sized but razor edged.

The DNA held during the early years of experimentation, however Mekhyr could not accept the combative nature of the line so continued until he perfected the breed surrounding them now.

Although unable to stop with the first group he was equally unable to destroy them so he made them outlying sentries below the equator and they were told pretty much the same story the rest were told. To keep them from travelling very far.

There were blowholes in this ocean that were a thousand times bigger and more dangerous than they were.

Unfortunately, there seemed to be a lot of unfortunates lately, one of their scouts had witnessed the Earther ships dive into Kyra and the scene involving Rianna.

It wasn't long before a team of the "bad boys" showed up banging on Mekhyr's door.

Gwyndolyn had returned home shortly before so was spared the ensuing free for all as they glared through portals and swam threateningly close to the maben ponds.

But when they finally made their way to the domes, there was no shielding the occupants from the failed experiments confronting them.

They felt like fish in a fishbowl as the Fen-Folk made faces and tauntingly tapped on the domes, acting like infantile teens in old Earther movies some had watched.

They popped into the bubbles here and there, startling occupants in rooms.

Chaos grew slowly throughout the city and the council called for an immediate meeting.

Meanwhile, the Muir-Gheilt gathered in a protective wide barrier around the maben ponds. Mekhyr guiding them from the confines, or safety as you wish, of the small craft.

The surreal circumstance playing out was so unexpected Aelwen wasn't sure what to do until it struck her during the Council meeting.

"We need to use the short jumpers. We can trap them in range of the jumpers and send them to the other end of Enceladus."

As the others murmured assent, she turned to the head of the jumper team, "Please set this up, Meijhr." He nodded and left, followed by a handful of council members too nervous to sit idly doing nothing.

Gwyndolyn entered the room as they were leaving. "Aelwen, what were they doing here?" She paused briefly, thinking ahead to a solution.

"The only way to remove these troublemakers is to force a jump back to the deep, Mother."

Gwyndolyn proudly observed her strong and intelligent daughter. "Well done, Aelwen." They left the room together and walked briskly toward the jumper station.

The timing of this fiasco couldn't have been worse. Aelwen tersely grilled her Mother for whatever she knew of the Fen-Folk surrounding them.

Gwyndolyn smiled and turned her daughter toward the tunnel they needed to traverse to reach the jumper station. Aelwen felt a momentary surge of power as she realized the relief hidden in her mother's actions and knew it would not be long before her mother was ready to turn the position as leader over to her.

She was ready with the certainty of youth and unending confidence in herself but she also felt the weight of the concept envelop her in a nearly suffocating embrace.

It made her slightly uneasy though, at the same time, she thrilled to the thought that she would be the one taking their civilization toward change.

With the advent of the Earthers, much change was about to occur. She squared her shoulders and gained a sense of direction she had not felt before and knew she would be ready.

The pair reached the jumper station and watched as the jumpers were deployed to various locations in the domes.

The Fen-Folk also watched, curious about the reason for this activity, not recognizing the jumpers as they had never seen them before, compliments of Mekhyr.

Mekhyr meanwhile had his hands full, or rather the mechanical arms were full of Fen-Folk he managed to grab as they swam by.

There were seven of them in the group harassing the city. With two in the grip of the craft, five were easily kept from the young.

Females ringed the ponds in three rows with two more rows of males surrounding those. The Fen-Folk were not getting through. Not with the Muir-Gheilt holding their plant tending pitchforks at the ready.

Four of the Fen-Folk lazily and arrogantly swam just out of reach taunting them and grinning to show off their razor-edged teeth. Laughing at the shudders and grimaces the Muir-Gheilt made in response.

"Yeah, yuk it up jerks", someone yelled. The group involuntarily drew back as the Fen-Folk pretend lunged at them, laughing hilariously, rolling as they held their sides.

"Idiots", another whispered loud enough for those around her to hear.

One of the Fen-Folk heard her and came within inches of the tines surrounding her as he snapped his jaws as though he would make her his next meal, growling menacingly.

She shrieked and hid behind the others. He swam off laughing louder than before.

Aelwen realized the only way this would work was if they could notify Mekhyr, letting him know he should release his captives and then they needed to draw the Fen-Folk away from everyone else.

They would likely have a small window of time to transport the unruly group before they mixed with advancing Muir-Gheilt.

She shared her concerns with her mother who raised a hand and closed her eyes, concentrating. She glanced out at the scene before them as Mekhyr released the two he still held.

She quickly explained to the jumper team and headed out the nearest airlock to be the bait. Gwyndolyn began to call her back but stopped and watched as her brave daughter swam out with her head bubble barely in place, to call the ne'er do wells to their fate. She only wished she could see their faces as they landed back in their own waters.

They swam toward her as planned and then she landed with them in their end of the ocean! Oh no. She let out a gasp. She got to see their faces alright and they mirrored her own.

Now she was the one surrounded and not by friendly faces.

Gwyndolyn looked stricken as she watched her daughter disappear and Mekhyr's eyes darkened in concern as he caught the forlorn glimpse of Gwyndolyn's emotional turmoil.

He didn't hesitate as he turned the craft and flew through the water toward the equator. The air in that bubble was not going to last for long and there were no domes in that end of Kyra. Though the instrument domes held air. If he could just get her to one in time. The craft had no air lock so he couldn't bring her inside. He could jump from instrument dome to instrument dome however.

The jumper team leader looked on in shock as he watched their future leader disappear with the dangerous group of Fen-Folk.

Snapping orders, he quickly came up with a plan. Sending a large group of Muir-Gheilt toward the equator, Meijhr cautioned them to take their weapons and do everything possible not to engage the Fen-Folk if it wasn't necessary.

"Remember, if you kill any of them they will retaliate. If you simply restrain until you are close to home, it will go better for all of us. But whatever you do, do NOT return without Aelwen." He watched them swim off and turned to Gwyndolyn. "We will get her back", he promised. She shook her head in agreement though in her heart she knew it would be Mekhyr that would return her daughter to her.

Mekhyr felt the fear and pain of Gwyndolyn the entire way. He knew she would never forgive him should he not bring her daughter back to her. He couldn't live with that. He would not fail her. What he felt for Gwyndolyn bordered on emotion and was the strongest feeling he had other than the need for preservation of his species.

The lights of the craft shone out searching for any sign of life and mile after mile went by as he flew on until he found them. They were circling Aelwen as she held still, petrified by fear and lashing out in panic alternately.

She was beginning to run out of oxygen. He knew this from the time that had lapsed and the bluish tinge to her lips as she exerted herself.

The nearest station was a kilometer away. He had just passed it. He maneuvered the craft into position to snatch her out of their midst as she gratefully realized he was about to rescue her. The Fen-Folk spread out to avoid the mechanical arm coming their way and she gave the last laugh as she went limp and was transported swiftly to air.

The trip home was uneventful until they reached the Muir-Gheilt rescue pod. They insisted she travel with them from there and amid much fanfare, her homecoming showed her how she was treasured by the ones she would soon rule.

Aelwen was more than ready for a rest as she was delivered to the airlock and she removed the bubble.

Gwyndolyn grabbed her in a fierce hug and moved her toward her home. "I thought we had lost you", she spoke low and relieved, voice thick with emotion.

Aelwen looked at her mother with love and leaned against her gratefully as she was ushered through another door to her bedroom and was made to lie down.

Gwyndolyn went around shuttering the room from outside light and closed the door behind her before going to see Mekhyr to talk about their plan for the Earther ship.

She was sure that, for the moment, the Fen-Folk would remain on their own side of the equator. Until they became curious enough about what had happened to them. Hopefully it would be a few cycles before then.

Mekhyr watched as she headed out of the airlock. She felt him search her mind and heart. For once she was grateful for his connection with her.

It reminded her, in many ways, of the link she had shared with Rhun. It was comforting. Her eyes brightened as she remembered.

Mekhyr felt joy at her happy memories and sad because he knew it drew her ever closer to the Rhun she remembered. Maybe one day she would see him the same way and let the memories go, making way for new happy living.

For now, though, they needed to focus on the task at hand and unless he was really careful he could lose her permanently. He met her outside and they walked together to the Earther ship. The first thing needed was a short lesson in flying it.

Gwyndolyn had had lessons enough to fly Mekhyr's ship. A series of lessons for every ruler in the event Mekhyr was no longer there.

The fleet could be activated if needed. She also knew how to fly the craft. In fact, she had gone with Mekhyr many times over the years to service the instrument stations. These monitored for quakes, water changes and temperature fluctuations.

It didn't take long to ready both Gwyndolyn and the ship. He followed her in the craft with a jump station he had installed immediately after his return with Aelwen.

His heart in his throat as she left through the hole in the icy crust, he followed her even there and locked onto her signal, clenching his jaw he transported her to the craft, leaving the Earther ship to traverse space pilotless, on auto and headed back toward Earth.

Maybe they would believe the two men perished and would take their time before returning to this area of the galaxy. In spite of the fears Gwyndolyn harbored regarding her short jump, it went without a hitch and he held her close for an all too short moment as she caught her breath. Letting her go only to take them back home.

CHAPTER TWENTY-ONE

Jeffrey gawked at the domes and inhabitants, noting mythlike creatures he was afraid to put names to for fear he had lost his mind completely.

Aaron all too readily put those names to the elves and fairies and the angel leading them through the city.

Jeff kept trying to shut him down but the adrenaline pumped through Aaron like blood through a heart. There was no shutting him up so Jeff stopped trying and tried to keep enough distance that he could try to assimilate the vision before them.

Of course, the inhabitants were likewise gawking at the two men from Earth. The chatter and rustling as they observed them was nearly deafening in the enclosed tunnel.

Mekhyr pushed a path through the crowd as he led the men to the Council Chamber. Gwyndolyn and Aelwen trailed behind trying to give calming answers to the ones gathered there.

Jeff was still mad at Mekhyr for duping them into drinking that knock out drug! He was going to be getting a solid piece of his mind as soon as things quieted down.

And the ship! Where was their ship? He didn't see it as they were led from Mekhyr's ship to the domes, bubbles on their heads, looking like ancient astronauts. Where was it? Far away or gone, it was inaccessible to them.

Aaron's head practically swiveled 360 as he tried to take everything in at once. This was eye candy to an engineer. The sheer magnitude of the underwater dwelling was inconceivable according to a human's concept of anything.

The guys back home would never believe them. Then he remembered. They had no ship to return in. The thought hit him hard and as he sobered he glanced at Jeff who obviously had already had this realization.

"Hey, Jeff", he called, "We are prisoners here." Jeff nodded glumly. The only stain on this otherwise incredible discovery was that they could not share it.

Aaron began to look a bit down too for a change. His conscience twinged as he noted that with a bit of satisfaction.

Then he edged closer and told Aaron "Look, all we have to do is fit in and figure out how things are done here."

More quietly he added, "Then we see what can be done to get back home. Ok?" Aaron started to smile and Jeff hushed him again with a shh, "Can't let on or we will never have any freedom here."

Aaron suddenly clammed up and Jeff didn't hear another peep from him until their meeting was well underway. He'd seen this before when Aaron had to work a serious problem out. It was like he withdrew into a place in his own head where he could visualize every aspect of the issue at hand.

He knew that if anyone could figure out the best way to get them home, it would be Aaron.

They turned a corner and Jeff was motioned through an opening into a rather large room with glass bubbles in the floor.

Weaving their way through these and the chairs, they reached the front of the room just as others began filing in.

Those entering the room hummed with excited communication about the new comers. They had always welcomed those from other planets when they made their way to their city but this was the first time Earthers had arrived.

Nairia was the first to speak as the last of them were seating themselves. "Aelwen, Gwyndolyn, Mekhyr." She nodded briefly at each in turn. "We saw you take their ship."

As usual Nairia was blunt and to the point as she cocked an eyebrow at the trio. "What are we doing now?"

She was correct. It was *them* as a whole, that were responsible for the actions that day. If anyone suffered for it, it would be all of them.

Mekhyr cleared his throat. "We are kidnapping the Earthers." He looked out at the roomful of Enceladans and almost smiled at the sea of shocked faces.

"We are not harming these two. Just accepting them into our city as one of us. They will eventually accept us as well, I am sure." He did smile then and moved to bring the two men forward.

"Welcome our new citizens." He stepped back and they all clapped politely as Jeff and Aaron looked at each other in complete surprise.

Nobody on Earth would admit things like this to their citizens! This was a foreign concept to them and neither knew how to deal with it at the moment. Maybe later they could understand better how it worked here.

About that time, Gria, the youngest fairy, several thousand Earth years old, fluttered up to eye level and blew a kiss at Jeff. The room erupted in laughter and even Jeff had to grin at the obvious attention.

Aaron just looked disgusted and muttered, "And he gets the girl again!" Aelwen looked askance at that but Aaron just smiled back wryly and she filed the info away.

Gria gave a little grin and landed on Jeff's shoulder and whispered in his ear. The flush started at his neckline and reached his hairline as the room erupted again.

This time, not even trying to be polite about it.

Jeff grinned helplessly and reached up to let her stand on his hand. She winked at him roguishly and flew away.

Aaron just shook his head in resignation and clapped Jeff on the back as he grinned too. She *was* impish after all. Who could help it?

They were the last to leave the room as everyone filed by individually to welcome them and introduce themselves.

Mekhyr had requested rooms for the two and assured them they would have bigger quarters as soon as they could be constructed and furnished.

The rooms they were shown to were lavish and expansive already, leading them to wonder just how large the permanent housing would be.

Jeff yawned and asked if they could rest now.

When they were left alone, Aaron finally spoke up. "We need to just fit in like you said, Jeff. Then we can talk. I want to see more and understand more about how they get around here, deal?" Jeff nodded wearily. "Nite then, Aaron." He headed in and fell into the cocoon bed. The floating sensation lulled him to sleep within a few seconds.

Aaron looked in on him and seeing Jeff lightly snoring, he found the bathroom then checked into his own cocoon. He fell asleep even faster.

Mekhyr and Gwyndolyn looked in on them and shuttered the sleeping areas then shut off the soft lighting, leaving only a few floor lights on.

"Do you think they will grow to like it here?" Gwyndolyn's voice was uncertain.

Mekhyr wanted to console her and say yes, but there was much to do between now and that eventuality. "Maybe, maybe not. We will see." She nodded and they went separate ways at the end of the hallway. Gwyndolyn to sleep and Mekhyr to deal with security around the jump stations. For he had caught some of the thoughts leading to the two human's private conversation.

CHAPTER TWENTY-TWO

Eljarren held the title of head of security for as long as he could remember. Even on Titan. That was a long, long, long time. It never meant much as there was nothing beyond the occasional squabble to calm or the breach of a seam to deal with.

Nothing truly bad had ever happened here. Until now. Eljarren was one of the remaining few elves and was, like the fairies, several thousand years old.

One tended to lose count at around 3000 or so. Usually that meant, if asked, that one was 3000 years old forever. But Eljarren knew he was closer to double that were he to be honest.

He still had a few tricks up his proverbial sleeve and could still conjure a bit of magic but mostly as a nudge for things happening naturally.

Changing the direction of nature required a bit more than he could spare. Most of his nudging went towards maintaining his own life.

So, when Mekhyr came to see him about the Fen-Folk and humans, Eljarren was quick to point out the fallacy of allowing him to lead the team.

Perhaps Mekhyr could appoint someone else for such an important detail. Someone like Gareth perhaps? Leaving himself to the daily needs of the city.

Mekhyr stood looking over the city and nodded, "Perhaps you are right then Eljarren. Do you know where Gareth is? He would be an excellent choice, being Muir-Gheilt but could you at least be his commander? He is still young and may need guidance on this. It is a dangerous mission. The Fen-Folk are a very aggressive species and will not hesitate to rip our gentler Muir-Gheilt to shreds. Perhaps you could accompany me in the craft if there is a confrontation?"

Eljarren nodded acceptance of these small concessions. After relating the need to keep their new citizens away from jump stations, Mekhyr excused himself and set out to locate Gareth when Eljarren said he thought he was at the distribution center delivering a load of sea vegetables.

And that's where Mekhyr found him half an hour later, having wandered through the various tunnels to the warehouse. He passed through the cleaning station where the workers were hosing the sea water off the produce, preparing it for the distribution center.

"Gareth", he called through the bubble mic. Gareth looked up and waved then turned back to the task he was completing.

When finished he went to the bubble saying, "What's up Mekhyr?"

Mekhyr squatted at the bubble, "Eljarren and I just had a discussion on added security." He didn't need to explain.

Gareth nodded agreement and when Mekhyr asked him to lead the team he readily took charge and accumulated the rest of his team. Happy to have Eljarren as a commander, because quite frankly, he wasn't a strategist. He could form the team and monitor the area and he could even rally them to fight and train them to do so but Eljarren was the one with the best strategies for anything and everything.

Mekhyr left him to it and headed for his ship. It was time to check the DNA banks. Nothing ever changed but the first time would make it the last time if he didn't act quickly.

Gareth met with his new team at the edge of the maben ponds. He nervously watched the darkness, listening for anything out of the ordinary.

He didn't know how long it might be before the Fen-Folk would be back. Hopefully the sudden jump would keep them disoriented for a long while. He waited for Eljarren to arrive.

He looked at the dozen faces in front of him. Hopefully they would be enough but just in case, he was making them each an assistant team leader and they could each recruit another dozen to help monitor the perimeter of the cities.

They spanned an enormous area but the hub was actually a point in the middle of the outer edge of a sprawled metropolis and the hub was the only place the Fen-Folk knew about for now.

They wanted to keep it that way. Tunnels leading to the others were buried. The other cities actually fanned out the opposite way, ultimately creating a rayed circle, however, half appeared to be invisible to those that knew of it.

In the center, the maben ponds were more protected here. From pollution, carelessness or outright vandalism, which was extremely rare. At least they used to be. Now they were in danger.

Eljarren finally arriving glanced at Gareth's choices. Baari, Engoldo, Daria, Faryen, Hamarre, Diarmuid, Grodna, Logori, Cairbre, Conn, Brighid & Opria, with her twins Kyne and Rylee.

All excellent choices. A strong mix of male and female. They would choose great Lieutenants and would handle their responsibilities with care.

He addressed them through the water mic. "I know each of you will do well. Gareth chose each of you for your calm intelligence, resiliency and ability to guide others. Now you each need to choose just as wisely. Your Lieutenants will also need to choose wisely. As you each grow your team we will have enough to cover our entire perimeter. You will each carry a radio with a sonar screen. If you see an attack on one of you, radio for help. We will alert teams of standbys in the cities at every guard station. These stations are 50 miles apart. You will each have 6 Lieutenants on either side of and in front of you. Each 5 miles apart."

"You each need backup so you will be half a cycle on and half off. Please see to it. If we do this right, we can repel within minutes. Don't leave your own station as they may try to draw you off to create a weak point."

The entire Muir-Gheilt population has been warned to stay within your perimeter.

He spent the next hour briefing them on the logistics portrayed on his waterproof map. Once they knew their station location they broke off and headed for the jump station. Some were going hundreds of miles away.

Gareth was scheduled to travel around the perimeter, fine tuning the process and training those in need of it.

He was the last to leave and headed straight for the guard station being erected nearby. Search lights were being fitted to the overhang facing both forward and to the sides.

A protective shield was built to keep the guard from physical harm while waiting for backup.

The local Muir-Gheilt were on alert and would help protect the maben. As he thought this the first wave of maben guards arrived. Each armed with a tined weapon of varying lengths.

Rhianna was with them. She swam up looking concerned and a bit afraid.

 She wanted reassurance but knew he could not yet give it so instead sought to assure him that they were ready for whatever would come. They had several groups of backups to call on if need be.

"I know you must go around the domes, Gareth", she eyed him with new respect and felt a surge of pride in her intended. "Gwyndolyn told me a little bit ago."

Gareth wondered how she could have known this, not realizing the link between Mekhyr and the ruler. "Yes, I have to leave in a few minutes."

He gazed longingly at the mermaid he loved and wished with all his heart he could be proposing marriage at this moment. She was so brave and desirable. He reached out to her, clasping her hand with his own. "Stay safe, Rhianna. Please don't engage in any fighting. Fall back and let the men battle if it comes to that. Promise me."

She adoringly looked into his eyes and promised. She had had her fill of danger for at least another cycle.

Gareth suddenly leaned over and kissed her full on the mouth. She heard coughing and soft laughter in the background as she flushed with embarrassment at the public display but couldn't help herself as she leaned forward for another.

The way he ran his hand down her arm as he took his leave left her with tingles in her belly. She wanted more. It was a good thing he was leaving.

She blushed again and he slowly smiled at the fetching effect. "See you in no time, Rhianna love."

Then he was gone. She vacillated between the thrill of him calling her love and the thought that he did it not knowing if he would return.

She swam a little twirl and when she finally opened her eyes found everyone glancing away quickly with little smiles tugging at their mouths, well most of them.

The jealous females were openly eyeing her with a full range of emotions. She couldn't help a little laugh as she swam to help build the shields for the maben beds. Soon enough even the jealous ones were pitching in.

Well it looked like they had declared themselves publicly.

She laughed again and tickled a little one under the chin, rewarded with a laughing gurgle and a tail in the air as the chubby little fingers grabbed for her hair.

CHAPTER TWENTY-THREE

The new guards sat in the seaside waiting room for their turn to jump, cracking jokes to ease the tension. "Did you hear the one about the…", his voice dropped off as he saw Gareth enter.

"Hey guys, ready for this I see." He nodded approval and whispered, "How does one get to the head of the line here? I need to get a head start on you guys to make sure everything is ready at each of your guard stations."

"Sure, you just want to be first in line", Baari joked, grinning.

Gareth pretended he was going to bop him on the head and grinned back. "Naw, just wanting to cut the odds on losing myself in that machine!"

He grinned again at the dismay beginning to show on their faces. "Not to worry guys. Just a joke of my own."

Laughing again he said, "Mekhyr tells me the last time they lost anyone was several annual cycles ago and it was only temporary. They have finally stabilized the jumpers."

As he headed through the door he muttered just loud enough for them to hear, "Of course that last one was never the same again." The door closed and he grinned.

Meijhr grinned back, having heard Gareth's parting shot at the team. "Funny man. They will get you back one day, you know."

Gareth shrugged, "It will keep things real. At least they aren't thinking about the Fen-Folk right now."

Meijhr motioned him to the underwater pad and Gareth obliged. "Starting with far side today. Riallo I think."

Meijhr smirked, "Hope you get there in one piece." He watched as Gareth's face fell, hitting the transport button. He chuckled, maybe he would think twice about making others afraid of the jumpers now.

Wasn't so funny with the shoe on the other, well with the… never mind. He shook his head and called next.

It was about time to take a break. There was an air hose for his bubble, but it was still a bother, and a break now and again was good.

After this one then.

One after another, the jumps went through without a problem. Meijhr realized he was holding his breath for each one. Well, so much for a break.

True it had been awhile but he only ever needed to use the machine once or twice a year as those like Svana went off world to visit family.

Engoldo went through, leaving Daria for last and Meijhr breathed a sigh of relief. Ready to call it a day, he motioned Daria forward.

She stepped up onto the small round platform and Meijhr turned the knob. There, that should do it. Stepping back, he read the monitor to confirm, picking up his things on the way.

Everything hit the floor as he realized this was the one time the machine erred. Oh, have mercy! Daria had two young ones and he had approved her against his better judgement because she was an excellent choice for lite guard duty. Daria was pregnant with her fourth child, having lost the third.

He *had* to get her back.

Flipping the switch to get Veloran City on the radio Meijhr barked out a code, retrieve, retrieve!

The radio static disappeared when Ajoro's voice came through. Rejected. Meijhr began to sweat as he began to adjust the signals and pulled back the essence that was Daria.

She began to materialize, slowly then disappeared again. Another adjustment and suddenly there she was.

Meijhr sat down and began to tremble at the thought that he had nearly lost her.

Daria, not realizing the danger she had been in swam to Meijhr and put an arm around him. "What is wrong, why didn't you send me to Veloran? Are you ok?"

Meijhr pulled his emotions in and squared his shoulders, patting her hand with his own. "No problem now, Daria but you won't be going to Veloran today."

Confused, her brows drew close together. "Meijhr?" He looked at her reluctantly. "I nearly lost you, Daria", he whispered in an agonized tone.

She drew back slightly then realizing he was truly shaken to the core, she leaned in again and hugged him. "But you didn't, now did you?"

Her matter of fact tone brought him round and he smiled briefly saying, "No, guess I did alright if you came back with that attitude!"

She smiled back, "There you are. Had me worried for a minute." "*I had you worried?*" he shot back. "I thought I was going to have to adopt your tribe to make up for losing their mother!"

Daria held still, the children. "Excuse me Meijhr, think I'll head for home then. See you tomorrow, ok?"

He nodded and raised a hand as she went out the door.

Gathering his things off the floor, he went out and locked the door. Time for a real break.

Last minute, Meijhr made a call to Eljarren. "Couldn't send Daria through. Almost lost her. Can you let Gareth know we will get her to Veloran tomorrow?"

Eljarren thanked him and he finally headed for home.

CHAPTER TWENTY-FOUR

Aelwen was more curious than ever about the two kidnapped men. Her duties led her away from home over the last few cycles and she hardly thought about them until returning during her normal sleep cycle.

She had been helping oversee the formation of all the backup teams in a dozen cities. She and Gareth shared what was happening through the dome bubbles so she knew what had happened to Daria before returning.

She spent the early hours talking with Meijhr and felt confident that he had corrected the problem. He did send Daria through the next day after all and Aelwen knew he would never have tried it if he hadn't fully believed it was safe.

At the outer airlock, she fitted the bubble to her head. They were being kept at the sister ship to Mekhyr's where only a fraction of one level was activated and accessible.

They were moved there, their first morning in the city as the novelty of Earthers proved overwhelming for their population. Maybe by the time their homes were constructed it would be better.

She had her concerns about that arrangement but didn't see any actual harm. She was more worried that they may try to venture into the ocean without a guide and find themselves in the clutches of the Fen-Folk. Or lost in the deep. Or worse yet, swimming out a blowhole to space, she stopped thoughtfully, *no that wouldn't be right even though it would solve their problem.*

It took her but a few minutes to cross to the ship Mekhyr lived in. He took her the rest of the way in the craft. Along the way she watched for any sign of the Fen-Folk but was rewarded with a glimpse of a school of fish instead.

She had rather hoped they would show while she and Mekhyr were in the safety of the craft for the long arms would have made short work of them. She didn't want them dead but would love to discover they were too afraid to come near anymore.

She had so many questions it was difficult to wade through the mental conversation to the one she wanted to have but Mekhyr brought their mid meal with him and she ate as the banter kept them from serious discourse.

In due course they arrived and she had her chance.

"We wonder why you are here ahead of schedule?" she blurted. Mekhyr winced. They would have to work on her Ambassadorial skills.

The two men looked at each other in surprise. "Ahead of schedule? How would you know anything about our schedule on Earth?"

Aelwen realized that were they able to return to Earth, she would have just given away the fact that they monitored Earth enough to know their secrets. Even their general public would not know this information.

How would she even explain interspace news to them? Most of the Galaxy knew everything about them. They were the favorite thing to watch as everything about them was ludicrous. Slap stick comedy except for the violence that was common to them, and the way they treated those weaker than they.

Aelwen sat on the edge of a console, pointedly ignoring the irritation on Mekhyr's face.

He might have her mother wrapped around his rules and regulations but she had no intention of following any other than her own in most cases.

Looking at Aaron, he looked like he might be more willing to divulge information, she asked, "What caused you to launch nearly five months in advance of plans?"

He had no idea how she knew but she obviously did so he decided to give her answers.

We discovered a way to stabilize wormholes for short distances and the knowledge that we could come here and return within a short period of time made the choice easy.

"Does anyone else know about us?" He blinked at that one. "How on earth could we? You guys live below the surface. Completely.

We almost went into shock when we saw that..that woman, fish, whatever that was, come flying out of the blowhole in the crust!"

"Muir-Gheilt", Aelwen stated. "Murr what?"
"Muir-Gheilt, merfolk". At his hesitation, she said, "Mermaids, mermen."

"Ohh, well that explains that." he was obviously being sarcastic. "How did our myths come to be reality here? In a freaking moon ocean?"

"Later", she said with a shake of her head. "You will have plenty of time to hear our story.

For now, I need to hear yours."

Aaron glanced glumly at Jeff. Well that answered that question. They really intended to keep them here.

Aelwen took pity on him and turned to Jeff as well. "Have you any idea how long it will be before they come looking for you?"

Jeff wanted to bluff through this but didn't think that would fly with Aelwen. She was too matter of fact to not see through it. Besides, she had some kind of intel on them.

"We unlocked the data aboard your ship", she shrugged at his startled look. "Did you think we were too backward to try?"

He had the decency to look embarrassed at least. She gave him credit for that. He didn't try to lie so got more points for that, too. But he still hadn't answered her.

"If you could answer my questions it will be to your benefit and if you would give us your codes, we will not damage your programs."

He looked startled again. If they had any chance of flying out of here they had to keep that ship intact.

He held a hand up in defeat. "No problem, just take us there and we will make sure you have complete access."

It was a good thing he had learned to play a pretty good game of poker. His face gave nothing away now. But inside a spark gave him hope. He might be able to send out a signal or set the system to only give a fraction of the information she wanted.

Enough for her to think she had it all, maybe. He didn't dare look at Aaron who glared daggers at him for so easily capitulating to her demands.

She quickly dashed his hopes. "Oh, we no longer have the ship. It is in space headed toward Earth. We are, however, accessing the ships systems to glean information."

For once, Jeff was speechless. He tried to mumble a yeah, sure and all his points went away as Aelwen knew with certainty that he had intended to deceive her. She would have done the same, in his place. After all they were prisoners on a strange world in an ocean and were fast losing hope of ever seeing their home again. She took her leave then and left them to lick their emotional wounds.

Mekhyr glanced at her in the craft, "So, did you learn anything?" He knew full well what she had gleaned from the encounter but wanted to hear it from her.

"Absolutely nothing and much." He nodded. "Go on."

"Well, they had no idea we existed but we need to access that ships data to ensure no vids were taken when Rianna flew out the hole."

She gritted her teeth at the thought and was more than a little irritated with her mother and Mekhyr for not checking before sending the ship away. The least they could have done was confer with her.

"Otherwise I learned they are not to be trusted until they are fully integrated. We will have to let them out sometime."

"Their homes will be done by cycle after next. I will find a few citizens to keep an eye on them at all times."

Mekhyr let it go for now. She still wasn't going to admit her fascination with these two. It would bear watching.

She was being responsible in questioning them and though he would have asked different questions she was learning quickly.

She was a great judge of character. Couldn't fault her there. She could see deceit easily. Aelwen would be a formidable ruler when her mother handed over that position. They had raised her well.

She took her leave at his ship and sought out her mother for a chat.

It didn't take long to find her. She was directing the Muir-Gheilt in their endeavors. Maben were being moved from the outer ponds to form a smaller area that would need protection.

The cries were deafening. Maben really didn't like being moved by anyone other than those they were familiar with. There were so many.

Seven hundred and ninety-nine to be exact. Four had just been moved over the last couple of cycles to the younglings who did not need constant care.

A flooded dome was being created to house those as it was the only way to protect them, inquisitive as they were. Vents were built in and pumps installed to keep water flowing.

Thara and Rianna were assigned to that group and were setting up a preschool to keep them occupied. This was so far removed from normal that they were instantly captivated and Rianna sat at one side surrounded on all other sides as she spun a tale of Fen-Folk.

Another detail was charged with creating an even bigger dome for the wee ones in the ponds. Both new domes were made with even sturdier materials than the city domes.

They could not be destroyed by anything other than what Earthers described as a nuclear device.

Fen-Folk were primitive and not technologically advanced enough to break into them.

The city domes were another matter, however, as they could be fractured with enough force. It would have to be repetitive but could be done.

At least 100 Muir-Gheilt would be housed with the maben for the duration of this emergency. The maben dome was set up like the youngling dome, with pumps and vents.

It would take another three cycles to complete both of these.

Well it looked like the Earthers could wait even longer for their own quarters as every available citizen of Kyra was helping with this project or in the guard.

So much for that chat! Aelwen really wanted that ship back. There was much to learn but the real reason was to ensure no videos of what had transpired outside the crust of Kyra would be available to Earthers when they found the ship.

Well it would have to wait but it couldn't be for long as it would be out of range by the end of next cycle. She would catch her mother at morning meal.

Pitching in, she worked until bone weary and headed for bed.

****

What was that awful din? Aelwen jumped out of bed and hit the floor running as the muffled cries and horror filled voices brought massacre to mind.

Unshuttering the room, she watched as people streamed by with fear-filled faces.

Some were attempting to calm those who were panicked while others shuffled along with a sense of dread showing in their movements, though some were probably barely awake.

She shuttered the room again and seeing no immediate danger, took the time to wash her face and dress before heading out the door.

"Aelwen", Tristan again! "What happened? Why is everyone headed to the South end?" Tristan looked grim which was new. He always had an air of nonchalance as though nothing could penetrate his barriers.

She stopped and looked him full in the face as her hand swung him around. "What is going on?"

His eyes took on a soft helpless anger and she could see moisture forming from his suppressed emotional state as he said simply, "I hear it's Thara. Found floating belly up near the domes." His voice quieted as he added, "Her body kept bumping along the dome. Pretty gruesome. She looked like something tried to take a bite out of her."

Aelwen paled and he quickly tried to take some of the sting out of the vision he had just painted for her in bloody tones.

As she tried to take a step back and began to slump with the weight of the loss and the terrible way it must have happened, Tristan reached for her and held her against him, comforting her with his steady touch and assurances spoken low.

Beginning to pull herself together, Aelwen stepped away and flushed as she realized she had not been grossed out by him this time. Well that wouldn't do. She began to walk with the crowd and realized he was trying to keep up.

They were not used to death like this. The occasional disappearance when someone went into the deep and never returned. Or when one who passed in their sleep was taken to Mekhyr for cremation in the furnace of his ship.

But violent death was not something they were aware of on Kyra. Surely it happened, especially with the Fen-Folk, but, that thought trailed off.

She suddenly stopped again, this time causing Tristan to nearly bowl her over. "The Fen-Folk. Could this be the beginning of an attack? Tristan were any Fen-Folk seen in the vicinity?"

Tristan's jaw clenched as he realized the implication. "I don't know, Aelwen. Let's find out."

They made it to the air lock sometime later and worked their way through the crowded area to the guard station.

Aelwen spotted Meijhr, and working her way over to him proved a bit risky as she narrowly avoided a collision with the gurney carrying her friend.

Emotions running like a seesaw, she grappled with the grief as her instinct to lead overcame her feelings. She had managed to lose Tristan along the way.

"Meijhr, what happened to her?" Her face showed little of the inner turmoil as she sought to understand the terrible things that were happening and tried to reconcile that with the need to bring order to the chaos.

He shrugged as he shot her a commiserating look. "We haven't determined how it happened yet, Aelwen, Mekhyr will let us know tomorrow."

Aelwen nodded. "Were there any Fen-Folk lurking around out there, Meijhr?"

He looked thoughtful as he looked up and said, "Not that I know of but again, Mekhyr should know. He has equipment set up everywhere and they scan the area."

As she turned to leave, he said suddenly, handing her an object, "We found this in her hand."

Aelwen turned the object over and over as she headed back toward her quarters.

It was a curious little thing. Tiny actually, and round. Nearly transparent and a gorgeous green with an odd hole through the middle of it.

Maybe Mekhyr would know the answer to this as well. She shook her head, troubled by the series of events set off by first contact with the Earthers.

Perhaps it was an omen. She wasn't superstitious but life had definitely taken a turn for the worse.

CHAPTER TWENTY-FIVE

Mekhyr glanced at her as she stepped through the airlock and into his lab. She hesitated briefly as she realized Thara's body lay on the hard table.

Steeling herself she looked away and looked at the object she brought with her, holding it out, "Do you know what this is?" He saw it and knew instantly what it was.

The Fen-Folk wore these gems in their hair. The brilliant jewels they were made of were mined from beneath Kyra.

He nodded, "It's a hair ornament. The Fen-Folk favor those." He stopped and looked at the fear in her eyes.

"Why?" Unfortunately, he couldn't read Aelwen like he could her mother. She answered uncertainly. "It was discovered in her hand", she nodded toward Thara.

Mekhyr came to a full halt then swung around to reach for the object. His thoughts drifted to a memory of the way the gems glittered in the hair of the Fen-Folk.

They were a fierce lot, cruel and unbending. Their females were nearly as violent as the males. Probably out of self-defense. He wished he had been able to correct the mistakes that made them the way they were.

Mekhyr sighed, "Well let's take a look at the area she was in." He went to his console and began replaying video feed. It took nearly a half cycle but he sat up and hit the switch, stopping the video.

Aelwen came over and peered at the dark waters near the station Mekhyr maintained along with the others. She found what had caught his attention.

A glimmer of color and a frantic face in the faint light from the station camera.

She glanced expectantly at him as he began to roll the video forward slowly and they watched as the fenman tugged on his captive with the seaweed rope her hands were bound with.

She flew at him with the force of his tug and the power of her flashing tail. She knocked him back and took a bite out of his face.

Aelwen gasped as she watched the gruesome scene unfold. Unable to tear her eyes away, she watched as her friend took the gash to her side from the edge of the station.

The fenman flew to her side and as he tried to hold her together, she grabbed at him in desperation and the gem slid down the strand of hair into her hand.

He was trying to tell her something and fear caused his features to lock in to a stony façade.

He began to swim with her in his arms toward the domes, looking into her eyes now and then until he realized she was gone.

Stopping, his eyes closed in resignation and he gave her a gentle push toward the nearest dome. Then swam back the way they had come.

The sadness in his eyes was powerful and spoke volumes about his lack of desire to hurt her. But he had.

Because of him her Thara was gone forever. Aelwen fought the anger, biting back the vicious words she wanted to hurl at the stranger on the screen.

Tears welled up making the already enormous azure eyes look even larger.

Mekhyr took pity when the tears began to make a trail down her cheeks and handed her a cloth to wipe at them.

She sat down and bending nearly in half, the sobs wracked her thin body as she finally gave way to the grief.

Mekhyr laid his hand on her shoulder and let her cry. It was good. She would be able to deal with this easier when done.

Aelwen shuddered with the raw river of emotion coursing through her. She wanted nothing more than to curl up and sleep but rulers could not afford that luxury.

She heaved a sigh and gulped in deep breaths, finally able to stand. "Thank you for letting me be."

Mekhyr nodded as he reassured her, "This will pass but for now perhaps it would be good to go back to your rooms and rest." He watched her leave and felt her sadness lingering in the room.

Going straight to her quarters for the second time in the last half cycle, she did finally curl up in sleep. Oblivious to the events outside.

Gwyndolyn quietly watched her daughter's journey home and noted her bowed head and slumped shoulders. She recognized grief having lived through her own.

Turning toward the crowd, Gwyndolyn gave guidance and consolation and what little information she had.

It was nearly a cycle before the group dispersed and she could head for her own bed. Nothing more could be done right now and the One knew she needed the rest.

CHAPTER TWENTY-SIX

Jeff stood still, observing the efforts outside. Surely this enormous undertaking was not to provide the quarters promised by the denizens of Enceladus.

"Hey Aaron," he motioned for Aaron to come to the window. "Check this out. Wonder what they are up to."

Aaron peered out the window and watching for a while, finally shrugged," Who knows. Too big for just us two, right?"

Jeff nodded thoughtfully, "What then?" he mused. Shaking his head, he watched a few more minutes, then wandered to the shelves at the back of the room. "How did these books end up on this water moon?"

He glanced at Aaron and back, "Keating, Tolkien, Milton, Tolstoy, Bradbury, Austin." These were just a few of the thousands of books lining these walls.

This was not the first encounter with those of earth, obviously. Other books were in languages of the stars. They had to be.

Symbols never seen on earth adorned their covers with images of places and beings he had no words for.

The most amazing were ten dimensional and defied explanation. Some spoke in the same languages when touched. Some played scenes out of nowhere into the middle of the room.

One, in particular, portrayed what must have been ancient earth. Before even the dinosaurs. Angels fought in an epic war. In the air, on the land, in space.

The planet was pitted and scorched by the time they were finished.

Why? Jeff was shocked by the violent encounter he witnessed. Where did they come from? Where did they go? What if they were real? What if they were not?

Visions of Mekhyr's wings led him to believe they were, in fact, real as life itself.

He shivered as truth hit him a solid blow. Nothing would ever be the same. How could you unlearn things like this?

Mythical creatures flourished here in this remote place. *As they had on earth.*

Mekhyr entered soundlessly and took in the wonder and revelations being realized. "Would you like to go to the city?"

Startled, Jeff turned to face his captor. Aaron had seen him enter and just grinned like the big goof he looked. "Count me in!"

Jeff nodded in agreement and they followed him to the airlock.

Fitting them with air bubbles, Mekhyr went first. Walking was a bit awkward, as before, but they soon got the hang of it and discovered they could pretty much float along.

As they entered the city, others tried not to gawk at them. Looking down or away. They knew the Earthers felt strange and out of place so attempted to treat them as if nothing was unusual.

And then there was Sioned. The regal elf strode toward them, completely unconcerned with their feelings.

" H'lo" Sioned bowed slightly in deference to their status as new citizens of Kyra.

"Where you off to, Mekhyr?"

"We are off to the gathering rooms to meet and greet." He smiled at Sioned, amused by the nonchalant indifference, even as he knew Sioned was ecstatic about the opportunity to converse with those from his birthplace!

"Well then, guess I will go there with you," He turned and matched his gait to theirs. He was a noble looking creature and Jeff could hardly keep his eyes off him.

Aaron wasn't faring much better. Fascination etched his features and Jeff couldn't help but smile as he noticed. Aaron was like a kid in Disneyworld.

Aaron cast a sideways glance to see how Jeff was taking all this, eager to share his exuberance, only to watch as his friend turned a bright red.

Curious, he turned to see what was affecting him in such a manner only to catch Gria, on tiptoe, whispering in his friend's ear again.

His chuckle caught the attention of the others and they looked amused as Mekhyr chided her gently, "Gria, perhaps you would stop tormenting our new friend and let him walk in peace?"

Gria looked petulant and endearing. Nobody could be upset with the fairy. She fluttered her wings and leapt off his shoulder to lead them to the gathering, looking every bit the miniature ambassador.

Put off by the excited females in the room, Gria disappeared into the woodwork, literally, to watch like the proverbial fly on the wall.

Jeff began to feel more at home with the attention. Looked like females everywhere were attracted to the opposite sex no matter where they were from. Nice.

Mekhyr's presence was required elsewhere and the two men were left to mingle and communicate at will.

Aaron found a group of engineers discussing the new domes and began to fit in as though he had always been there.

Jeff was drawn to the beauty outside the domes once again. He stood near the edge of the room viewing the maben ponds with their strange glowing aura.

The colors reminded him of a kaleidoscope with infinite colors and patterns that flowed. Though not fractal. Peaceful and invigorating all at once. He was entranced by the Merfolk.

He had always been partial to mermaid stories and wondered what it would be like to live in the sea more than once.

Embarrassed by his fascination, he hid it from the age of twelve. Now, he had to wonder if he had withdrawn into his own mind and gone quietly into the state of dementia his great aunt enjoyed. Completely oblivious to reality.

Watching the merfolk outside he decided he would at least enjoy the experience, real or make believe.

A voice near his knees woke him from his daydreams and he looked about searching for the speaker, finally looking down and squatting, he studied the greenest eyes he had ever seen.

Hair as red as any in Ireland, the mermaid bewitched him on the spot. She smiled seductively as she read him and knew his thoughts.

Singing out, taunting him to join her, she backed out into the open water and floated upright, holding his gaze and his adoration.

"Nairia!" Aelwen admonished her friend, "Don't you have enough mates and children?"
She laughed at Jeff's surprised response. "The Muir-Gheilt do not age like we do. Nairia there is approximately 2000 earth years old.

"Don't know if I can get used to this." He muttered distractedly, looking anywhere but at the one who had nearly lured him to her part of this moon.

Aelwen laughed again, "You will." She raised an eyebrow at him, "Want to go back out there?" His heart lurched and he gave a solemn nod, ever the stoic no matter what he felt.

She led him to the nearest airlock and fitted him with an air bubble, adding additional air bags to a backpack.

Putting her own bubble and pack on, they left the dome and entered Kyra.

Jeff was mesmerized. For the first time he could take as long as he wished to just *view* the merfolk and the maben ponds.

"Why are they building a dome around the coral beds?" he glanced at Aelwen who merely headed that direction so he would follow.

As they arrived at the edge of the coral, Jeff could clearly see they were indented deeply and held the cutest bunch of babies he had ever seen.

All with tails and gills. A tether of seaweed attached to the tail kept them from swimming off but now and then as a tether broke he saw an adult race off after the gurgling baby who squealed with laughter when caught.

"Oh." "Well why don't you move their dome closer to the city?" It made perfect sense to him to have the vulnerable more accessible.

He saw that apparently Aelwen didn't see the same logic when she smiled as though at a toddler, "Don't you feel the temperature difference here?"

Of course, hydrothermal vents must be in the area.

"Heat and nutrients!" Jeff began to *really* look at the area. "There!" he pointed at the slightly different plume of water, and "There!" She watched, suddenly interested in his show of understanding.

"But doesn't the ocean itself contain the same nutrients? And you could artificially heat another area, right?

"We could, she agreed, but they, she waved, would die." A puzzled Jeff turned to study the coral again. Maybe he had missed something? Turning back to Aelwen, he remained confused by her statement.

She wavered between not trusting and trusting this earther with a fundamental aspect of survival here.

She wasn't quite ready to divulge that information after all, "It has always been this way. Why change it now?" She turned away, hiding the lie on her face, remembering the package implanted centuries ago.

Jeff wasn't convinced but knew that eventually the truth would out. For now, it was enough to be here.

Wandering closer to the workers and the portion of the dome already finished, Jeff wove between the maben ponds and as he neared the center he sensed something magical but fleeting. Shaking his head, he realized that he hadn't eaten in quite a while. "Do you people eat at certain times or is it whenever hungry?" Aelwen smiled, "Whenever you're hungry you go to the dispensers."

"And those can be found where?" His eyebrow rose. "Just off the common areas in the dining halls. Come on, I'll show you."

They headed back toward the airlock. As they approached the halls she spoke of, Sioned made another appearance and Jeff wished he could turn and go back.

That elf made him feel downright awkward. Maybe it was because he was wafer thin and was made of at least 7 dimensions. It was enough to make a person ill just to watch him move.

No wonder they were mythical on Earth. Nobody could get a clear glimpse of them. They defied light and substance though they were very real and *present*. He blinked.

Well maybe he was wrong about the real part. Suddenly Sioned was no longer there. Then just as suddenly he reappeared with another elf at his side.

Aelwen began to laugh at the astonished look on Jeff's face. At first he looked at her, confused by the humor and then glared as he began to feel he was the brunt of a joke.

She shook her head. This was funny but their guest was feeling embarrassed. "We have never been able to determine how they do it and they have never been able to explain to us in a way that we can understand."

"They just seem to go wherever they desire when the thought becomes *solid*. That's the only way to explain it."

Ruefully she, once again, wished they knew more so they could engineer a way for all of them to do the same. If Mekhyr knew, he was never going to tell them.

Jeff sped up briefly as he called out, "Aaron! Over here. What have you been up to?"

Aaron grinned and came to greet his friend. "You wouldn't believe how they build things here! Fascinating stuff. Kind of glad we are trapped here so I can pick their brains."

Jeff grinned back. Some things never changed.

Something Jeff *had* noticed when the elves or fairy were near was a kind of tingling power felt by every sense and every nerve in his body. The same kind of tingling he felt by the maben ponds.

"Well look who's here," Aelwen sauntered up to the center bubble, stunned by the fenman's audacity.

He looked at the anger in her eyes and began backing away as if she could destroy him with her thoughts.

Aelwen scanned the room quickly, looking for anyone inhabiting another bubble. Seeing no one she turned back to the murderous fishman. "You certainly have nerve! You murderer! You killed my friend."

Her voice became a shrill wail as she flailed at the bubble, losing control for the first time since losing her father.

Sioned stood in shock at the scene as Jeff reached her side in a flash.

Grabbing her hands he looked into her wild eyes and spoke instinctively, "Shhh, Aelwen, we have to find someone to help," he held her against himself and marveled at the sensations assaulting his mind and body.

He stepped away but continued to hold her hands, maintaining eye contact until the wild anger left her.

By then, the fenman had gone.

Aelwen sank weakly into a chair feeling embarrassed and furious and helpless all at once. The force of it surged through her, ripping her apart as she fought to create a plan of action.

Aaron, for once, looked lost and sat too, unable to speak to the situation, he gladly let Jeff handle it.

CHAPTER TWENTY-SEVEN

Gwyndolyn let the last of the workers go. A fresh crew would be there in a few minutes.

Tidying up the area and placing dropped tools on the makeshift benches, she glanced around the ponds and wondered if maybe this temporary change would become permanent.

They had never been restricted here other than for the need of air and living in the domes. Even that allowed freedom with the water bubbles but even the limited freedom allowed the maben, as they left their beds, would be gone.

The forays into the edges of the deep were no longer safe. The claustrophobic feelings constricted her throat but pragmatic as she was, it was gone as quickly as the thoughts invaded her mind.

She gazed into the domed city, waiting for the new workers. As her eye followed the hallway to the communal area, she realized Aelwen's distress and was at the airlock without realizing she had moved.

En route she caught peripherally a splash of brilliant color, instinctively racing toward it. She came close enough to grab at the fenman's tail, causing him to spin and hiss in distress.

Fearfully he peered into the area around them, looking for any reinforcements. Seeing none he became a little bolder and lunged at her, then pulled back.

"I am sorry, I meant no harm to the pretty one. I felt," he looked awkwardly at the ocean floor, "I felt", he lifted a fist and tapped on his chest with it, "need for her," he finished softly, looking at her with a need to be understood.

Clearly, he had been watching them from the deep enough for Gwyndolyn to suddenly feel violated and fearful herself however his meaning penetrated the fear and she realized he had fallen in love with Thara.

He had attempted to kidnap a mate! With the implications sinking in, her face portrayed the sadness and pity she felt for his loss.

He slipped away into the deep as she watched, feeling so vulnerable.

Mekhyr watched it all then sat back and contemplated the events. On Titan there were episodes like this.

When DNA became corrupted and so many lost control of their ability to empathize. This was only different in that it happened because of love and much empathy.

The lack of societal skills in the Fen-Folk were his fault and he felt the brunt of that cleave through his heart, knowing Thara's death needn't have happened. The pain of her loss rippled through their little community like a tidal wave.

Bowing his head, he let the rare emotions overcome him and then stood and turned out the lights and headed for the bedroom he never used to find a place of peace and quiet, needing to meditate on his Creator.

Entering the darkened room, he chose to leave the lights off and instead, lit a handful of candles then wandered to the porthole for a moment before settling into a familiar pose on the floor. Holding his head high and letting go the stress, Mekhyr let the hurt go with it.

Looking between the images in his mind and focusing on the light he found there was natural to him. He knew that light well.

Then he was in Parani viewing the home of his brothers and sisters, the fallen. Always on the outskirts of their inheritance. Always fighting to survive the banning long enough to convince their maker of their good intentions.

Empwyn looked up in surprise, noting the energy signature of her friend as he hovered in the ether surrounding her.

"Mekhyr!" Empwyn's exclamation caught the attention of several others in her vicinity. They gathered round, hoping to hear positive things from their emissary on Enceladus.

They had created a place as magical as Kyra though more reminiscent of the heavens they lost.

He soared high above them to see the extent of it. Shimmering atmosphere held the same magic sheen but the living spaces were more open, unencumbered by the need to separate air from water.

Thought provided privacy to the inhabitants of this plane. Though rarely was privacy necessary among those who had experienced life in the heavens of the One. Nothing was unseen there. Nothing was unknown. And though they had spent a trillion lifetimes on other planes and in other planets, the need for the openness haunted them.

He dove for the gathering and entered Empwyn's mind. She smiled and hugged him then leaned back to look into his eyes. Concern etched her forehead with faint lines. "It has been long since we've had the pleasure of a visit from you. Have you finished with the genomes already?"

"Not yet, Empwyn. I have some difficulty on Enceladus. I lost Thara. You needed to know. I am so sorry." He held her as she shuddered and grasped his robe.

"There was no way to reclaim the genome? I've lost him forever?" The sad nod told her everything she needed to know. The faint trace they retained of her mate was gone.

There had been the smallest hope that, over time, they would clone and replace the clone's dna with that of her beloved.

Suddenly Mekhyr found himself ejected as Empwyn felt the need for such privacy as he had been thinking of.

The others saw her need and wandered away, mystified by her reactions but knowing she would eventually share.

Slowly becoming aware of his surroundings, Mekhyr sighed. Too much sorrow. He needed to make a trip. Rising, he snuffed out the candles, noting the waxy scent. Heading out the door he turned toward the airlock with the small craft.

CHAPTER TWENTY-EIGHT

When building the domes, the engineers had been tasked with creating islands under the natural domes of the moons crust. Many honeymoons were enjoyed here. There were actual walls both above the water and in the water.

The center of these structures contained quarters to Mekhyr's specifications. He could see out, nobody could see in, however he opted out of seeing into other private quarters. This was, after all, a place for newlyweds.

The outer area up to the crust was bioengineered to replicate the skies of Titan. Complete with Saturn with its rings, Dione and Enceladus as well as the sun and stars.

At night the beauty was nearly unbearable. Centuries of recordings played out one day and night at a time here.

It was the only place here that Mekhyr truly felt at ease and could regain his sense of wonder and renew his motivation to return home after centuries of depletion at the domes.

He just disappeared as far as the rest knew. He was usually gone for up to 30 daily cycles at a time and about every 36th annual cycle span.

Choosing not to announce his destination so the others inhabiting the island would not feel watched.

Making his way into this inner sanctum was much like entering the underwater space of any rig under the oceans of Earth.

He simply guided his craft into an inner pool and opened the airlock, stepping onto a platform and making his way into his suite of rooms.

Here, in his secret place, was a room full of all the latest lab equipment and technology of the Universe. He was in his element as a geophysicist and geneticist.

As an Angel, all he must do is think it and it was. Until the Falling. They retained many powers but lost many more.

Each time they used the powers they had, the more they lost physical cohesiveness. This reinforced the need for even more research and experimentation.

This was also the repository for the duplicated of the *packages* stored onboard his ship.

Hydrothermal activity was focused and consistent here and powered the island including his cryogenics station.

Mekhyr entered and began installing the packages he had accumulated. There were pitiful few considering the years it took to collect them.

When those carrying them were as long lived as the Enceladans.

If he only didn't feel such empathy for them he would have been gone by now but he couldn't doom them to death in such a way.

However, if he could just find a way to get what he needed *and* leave them intact! That was his current goal and he was halfway there.

He had reviewed the process, this far, so many times he no longer needed to add it into the equations visually.

He searched the written portion once again, catching the same tiny hint of the direction he needed to take this.

Setting a slow and deliberate pace for himself he began the tedious work.

Bringing his captive out of stasis was the first step. This one was one of his earlier mistakes. The war within over his use of this being was intense. It broke every high principle he lived by otherwise.

The only exonerating factor was that he would have destroyed this one with the rest of his mistakes.

Darkness pervaded this part of his life and it was the only thing he was too ashamed to divulge to Gwyndolyn. Guarding this area of his mind was a constant reminder of his betrayal. Not just to her but to the *real* Creator.

Only the short-term wakening saved him from the worst of the guilt. His subject was alert for moments before sedation for the surgeries. Then the moment he came out of that he was engulfed in the stasis field till the next time.

Surgery was as unsuccessful as all the others but Mekhyr noticed that the genome package lasted moments longer before showing signs of distress.

Securing it in another stasis chamber, he began the calculations necessary for every change in the normal course of things, defined by previous results.

Meanwhile, Gwyndolyn paced in the ship wishing there were a way to let him know of the encounter with the fenman.

She waited into the night cycle hoping he was only out on patrol. Finally deciding the wait was futile, she went back to the dome.

Aelwen was gone, having formed a security detail to trace the fenman back to his lair. This time taking a water sled with as many air packs as she could load on it.

Eljarren sent word to Gareth of the events and Aelwen's mission. Hoping he could reach her in time to provide support and protection.

Gareth gathered as many guards as were in the vicinity and sent word out that more should head toward the part of Kyra that had suddenly become such a popular destination.

His quickly assembled pod flashed through the water. Streaking toward their next ruler.

Nobody could reach Mekhyr. Gareth was worried. Would they be able to deal with this without the Ancient?

He had been working without rest for the better part of five cycles by then and now this. The Muir-Gheilt needed little sleep but did require rest at intervals regardless. His need to do so was great.

CHAPTER TWENTY-NINE

Aelwen kept her little guard moving through the darkness of the water as the darkness was broken only by their pathetic torches. Seeing only a meter in any direction. Not knowing who might be watching them from the depths. They were too visible, however none were willing to give up sight, except those who scouted for them with their sonar.

The occasional thrown shellfish assured her they were being watched but nobody showed themselves. She shivered with fearful apprehension and knew she should have waited for more guards to arrive.

Fortunately, she did not order the torches turned out. For it was by the glimmer of light that Gareth finally tracked her down and, in the process, located a handful of her tormentors. Dragging them into the light the group of travelers gaped at the colorful creatures. Their hair was not flowing like the Muir-Gheilt.

It was held in locks by round gems and crystals strung along the strands of hair. They had darkened eye rims with brilliant colors around that and one, the youngest, glowed very faintly. Just enough to be seen when within a few armlengths.

Gareth pushed that one forward and gratingly spoke, "Say you are sorry!" To Aelwen, he whispered, "This was the one lobbing shellfish", nearly grinning.

The defiant little one snarled back refusing to do as told. Gareth shook him slightly and put his face directly in front of his, "DO. IT. NOW!"

Taken by surprise at the authoritative voice, the youngest quickly stuttered, "I I I'm ssorry." Ducking his head, he withdrew to what must be his mother as she wrapped her arms protectively around his shoulders. He couldn't have been more than 1 full cycle grown. He wondered if they aged as quickly, to adulthood, as the Muir-Gheilt.

Aelwen graciously bowed her head in acknowledgement sending a fleeting encouraging smile in his direction. She let her gaze wander up to the one who appeared to be their leader. A man! Of course, put men in charge and you get death and mayhem, she couldn't help but think this as she pondered the reason they were here and the pain gripped her again. It was getting lighter each cycle but was still intense.

The fenman's eyes were hard and dark and glinted with unfathomable hatred. It struck her like a fist. Recoiling, she fought to maintain her own equilibrium. "What is your name?" Aelwen demanded harshly. These fenmen seemed to emanate cruelty and the only thing they would respect is equal measure. When he failed to answer she followed Gareth's example and got his attention with her face as close to his as the bubble would allow. Staring him down, he finally snapped out, "Malik."

"What is your position, Malik?" She snapped back. If he was surprised he did not show it. "Head of my tribe."

Aelwen stepped back confused. Tribe? Apparently, the Fen-Folk had no structured governing body. Primitive.

But equally easy to take control of as they likely warred among themselves, she hopefully mused.

Turning to Gareth she nodded and he took charge of the little party, both fenman and their mixed group.

"Where is your tribe located?" he barked at Malik. More comfortable with a male asking the questions, Malik shrugged, "This way." He led them deeper into the dark waters.

After a couple of air bag replacements Aelwen noticed a faint light in the distance. Growing brighter as they travelled toward it. The nature of the community was a surprise as well.

A scattering of glowing crystals among resting places and places for play or work turned out to be the source.

Malik was also the leader of the community judging by the deferential nods as he passed them by.

They respectfully kept their distance from the entire group although the occasional child darted up to Dari, as Aelwen had learned was his name.

They hurriedly asked questions and got whispered replies before darting away again.

After the third such encounter, Aelwen began to grow uncomfortable. For some reason it was becoming clear that these young maben were actually part of a recon force.

They were taking information ahead and Aelwen's detail would become the prisoners upon arrival. Pulling back she drifted closer to Gareth, looking anxiously into his eyes.

He knew why as he had been watching the same interactions with great interest.

This *tribe* acted like a well-oiled machine and every part counted. In order to learn what they could they couldn't back out now and their best hostage was some distance ahead of them.

If they tried to run he was sure they would be overcome in no time and things could be much worse for them.

Smiling as reassuringly as he could, he hoped they would return safely to their home.

With Mekhyr gone, there was no real help coming. Only more small groups as they were told of the need. Easily overcome groups.

Gareth turned in circles looking for any openings in the crowd amassing behind them.

"Faryen", he called softly. As Faryen slid over and became close enough to hear, Gareth whispered a few words and suddenly Faryen disappeared with the nearly invisible speed of the Muir-Gheilt, taking everyone by surprise.

As he vanished, several of the Fen-Folk followed him, much slower.

Odd, thought Aelwen, she would have to ask Mekhyr about that. She had seen Faryen's ability to outdistance most of the other Muir-Gheilt in races they were so fond of holding.

She had no doubt he would succeed at whatever Gareth had instructed him to do.

Malik suddenly appeared in front of them as the crowd came closer, encircling their group. "You will stay here." He swept his arm toward the empty space ahead.

There were manacles of sorts attached to thick ropes of seaweed.

Placing one on an ankle or tail of each captive, the Fen-Folk in their group swam off with Malik, the youngest making a face and giving a wiggle of his tail as they left a handful of Fen-Folk to circle and watch over them.

Fortunately, they left her air sled with her. Unfortunately, there were only ten bags left. It took 3 to get there. She had approximately 2 cycles to spare.

Gareth followed her eyes to the bags and doing some calculations of his own, decided it was time to put a plan of action together.

"Hey!" He gestured for one of the Fen-Folk to come closer. "When will Malik be back?" All he got was a shrug in response and a smug grimace. Frustrated but patient he called out, "We need to eat."

As the fengirl disappeared, he hoped it would be to return with sustenance. They needed strength for the cycles ahead.

It was good that the only air breather was Aelwen based on the few bags left but he would give anything for it to be someone other than their next ruler.

A stir among those in the community caused ripples all the way to their circle, bringing with it a fenman who arrived, took Aelwen's manacle off and dragged her along behind him.

She lost her grip on the air sled and Gareth barely caught the line as it floated by.

He could see she fought to overcome the fear. "Aelwen," his voice broke through the clamor in her brain. "Try to relax. You will use less air."

She nodded and he sank gratefully to the ocean floor to wait. By the looks of her bag she had about 2 hours left in the bag on her pack.

If she struggled it could easily be gone in under half that time.

He wondered if Faryen had encountered other of the guards yet. As fast as he could swim, Gareth wouldn't be surprised. The way the Muir-Gheilt could move was pure magic. Gifted them out of the special heavenly powers retained by the Ancients it was so astonishingly out of the norm that the outward appearance of it fell within the unknown realm of magic.

He'd heard the name of this gift once, long ago and no matter how he tried he mangled it. It seemed that only the Angels could produce the necessary vocals to say it properly.

CHAPTER THIRTY

Eljarren waited nervously in the airlock as the guards accumulated. Not nearly fast enough as far as he was concerned!

Sioned stood calmly next to him and explained to the group of engineers outside what he needed to be able to accompany them to the deep. Even he did not know where it was Mekhyr disappeared to or he would get him now.

The best he could do was give aid with whatever little magic there was at his disposal. Other than for relocation, it had been long since he had even tried.

There they were. Several smaller groups had already headed out and he was concerned for them but was held up at the jump station bringing in those from other cities.

"Brighid," he left the air lock and greeted the warrior like merwoman. She looked fierce and she was the one who always won the wrestling matches. Even against most of the mermen.

He chose her to lead this mission as most everyone respected and admired her. They needed the cohesive team this allowed.

She stepped up, "Lo Eljarren. Checking on status of the mission. Looks like we are ready to go. Supply sleds will be here in a moment or so."

He nodded, "Good. Did you grab enough extra airbags to get Aelwen back from wherever they are?"

At her nod, he sighed. It wouldn't matter if she ran out of what she had before they tracked her.

This was frustrating. For the second time in just a few days, their next ruler was in need of saving.

Made you wonder if she was right for the role. Shaking his head, he re-entered the lock and headed back to the jump station.

Brighid watched him go and looked the guards up and down. "Who will bring the supply sleds?"

Seeing a show of hands, she went down the line, "Elrin, Myra and Brigio. The sleds have just arrived. You can each tow three. One of the sleds holds air for Aelwen. Don't lose it!"

They hesitated then Brigio stepped up to that sled and took the line. She took two more of the sleds that held nothing but fresh torches and headed for the line.

This line would sweep the most area in the least amount of time. Just more than an arm's length apart they would make a line at least a meter long.

Each held a torch. Each torch would last for two cycles.

Myra took the two holding food and one holding medical supplies. Elrin took the one that was three sled sizes and carried Sioned and his air bags.

The line finally started moving forward. Lights shone into the dark deep and they sang out to each other as excitement gripped them.

None of the Muir-Gheilt had ever been involved in war so had no idea what could happen. Sioned hoped that would not change on this trip.

Aelwen was innocent of war as well, though she, at least, studied it extensively as part of her rulership training.

Not only did she study Earth's history, good, bad and indifferent but also that of as many planets and dimensions as they had recordings of.

While earth children watched Cat in the Hat, she cut her eye teeth on Genghis Kahn.

Half cycle into the march the line wavered and halted. As bright as the lights were, he could see Faryen clearly.

He was speaking agitatedly to Brighid and her personal guard. The looks on their faces told him Aelwen and her guard had run into serious trouble.

The line began to forge ahead from the center. He watched as the guard linked hands and fell into an arrow shaped wedge. Lights went out for everyone but the tip of the line.

Brilliant strategy, Sioned smiled. Brighid was the right choice.

As they swept forward and encountered Fen-Folk they were taken behind the line.

As they met up with the guards Faryen had waiting, they joined the line, prepared to sweep around any enemy that showed itself on Brighid's command.

Very effective maneuvering for someone unschooled in war. She may make a phenomenal emissary on trips to other planets. He would have to talk with Mekhyr.

With the loss of Rhun, they had also lost the previous emissary. Rhun was good! Better than most he had known.

Understandably, Gwyndolyn had not been in a rush to replace her love in his governmental capacity. He feared at this point that only he and Mekhyr would ever fill it.

Now the idea was real, he was happy to realize the potential for continued interaction with some of the societies they had to place on hold.

He pulled out the hair bauble from his robe pocket and rolled it around on the palm of his hand thoughtfully.

So many on other planets found such gems as this to be extremely valuable and were willing to pay a great deal for them.

He returned it to safe keeping and watched as they found more Fen-Folk and as they melted through the line and into the group behind the line with the rest.

A ruckus broke out near the head of the line and Sioned tried to see what was happening through the roiling water and flashing of tails.

It appeared they had arrived in the community holding Aelwen and Gareth. The natives had become embroiled in a fight with their guards.

The tails of the line swung around and easily encircled the encampment three guards deep.

The worst of the noise and fighting centered around Aelwen. She stood with a fenman who held a knife to the line of her airbag. He was threatening everyone with her death if they didn't back off.

Sioned donned a bubble and airbag and suddenly appeared at Aelwen's side. Just as suddenly, he, Aelwen and the man with the knife were all in his little sled powered giant bubble.

He easily removed the knife from the grip of the fenman in a state of shock and distress.

Sioned quickly returned the fenman to the water and was back with Aelwen in a heartbeat. Helping her remove her bubble, he seated her on the one small chair he had insisted on.

"Are you going to be ok?" Sioned raised an eyebrow in concern. "Here, have a little water."

She shakily raised the bag to her lips and drank. "Thank you Sioned. What a nasty little fish!"

He chuckled at her descriptive vehemence. "Yes. Not very pleasant, are they?"

Looking out at the group again, he could see that his actions had triggered a willingness to give their attention to Gareth and Brighid.

It helped that they were surrounded on all sides including guards circling like sharks above.

"They are experiencing a bit of trouble themselves now, "He looked over his shoulder at Aelwen who brightened considerably as she realized the turnaround then blanched as she saw the wall of Fen-Folk coming from beyond, led by the pesky elder maben!

Ohh if she could just get her hands on those snotty brats!

Sioned was amused when he realized she was fighting mad though he wasn't sure what brought that reaction out. Didn't matter.

They were about to get slammed so he did the only thing an elf *could* do. He created a barrier that completely surrounded them, much like his sled bubble but bigger. Much, much bigger.

With no warning, the horde of Fen-Folk slammed into the barrier. It wasn't pretty. The first to hit were trapped and squashed by the rest who didn't realize they needed to pull back.

One or two Fen-Folk were obviously destroyed, and many had mangled body parts, ripped fins and bruised faces.

Aelwen sat in awed shock as she witnessed the amazing power Sioned sent out and the destruction that power wielded.

Never before had she seen damaged bodies such as these and she gagged as she tried to avert her eyes.

Then the surreal scene took another twist as the bubble reversed and trapped the horde, leaving the original group free to move about.

They left the larger group in the bubble and headed back with the smaller group, in which they located Thara's murderer, Kayrun.

Aelwen thought she would feel relieved but found herself feeling sorry for their captives, especially when she realized the similarities.

He had kidnapped Thara and killed her by accident. They had just kidnapped several members of his tribe along with him and killed or mangled others and they were not guilty of anything but protecting themselves.

They had also just left a larger number in a bubble. "Sioned?" she called to him as he stood on the other side of the sled bubble.

"Yes." He looked over at her, pleased to see she had abandoned the pallor and was once more herself. "The bubble?" She looked back at the Fen-Folk and then back to him.

"Oh that." He laughed. "Only long enough for us to get home and then release the other members of Kayrun's group."

She sighed and sat back. It was going to be a long couple of cycles. She saw a few cushions on the floor and decided to catch a nap while she could. Yawning, she curled up and slept as though dead.

Sioned even checked on her a couple times thinking, she must have been exhausted to show weakness to her people.

Several of whom swam by looking understandingly at her slight form. They paced the bubble, designating themselves her guards for the time being.

It was a good thing she was asleep, Sioned reflected as he watched the disgusting eating habits of the Fen-Folk on the trip home.

As the young girl licked the hapless fish and grinned with delight at his look of horror, her jaws dislocated and she swallowed it whole. Her jaws returned to normal and she licked her lips then, laughing at him as she swam away.

CHAPTER THIRTY-ONE

Aaron examined the new quarters from stem to stern and marveled at the craftsmanship in the utterly seamless dome.

While he watched the building of it avidly, he learned little of the techniques used.

One thing he did witness, far enough away he was sure his eyes played tricks on him, was what must have been the raising of the glass wall panels. Try as he might, he could not find the end of one panel.

Jeff watched him worry at the puzzle like a cat with a toy drenched in catnip! Well at least one of them had something distracting from the intense boredom.

He had played with the wall controls until Aaron asked him to stop saying it made him dizzy. There were apparently thousands of scenes built in to the remote.

Some included the strangest music, some were nature sounds but obviously not from earth. The scenes were not from earth either, but from what appeared to be Titan. Eerie and beautiful beyond words.

They came across the water dispenser by accident as it was all of glass with the source, a tiny opening, in the floor along the curve of the wall.

It was completely transparent until you touched it, then water flowed up the column and into a tiny built in basin to return down the same column in a separate channel.

The restroom was substantially more obvious with a toilet closet and a shower head over a floor drain. The walls were fluid and opaque, full of brilliant color.

Bed cocoons floated opposite each other with another semi-wall in the middle, filled with the same flowing colors, affording some semblance of privacy.

A couple enormous glass floor vases were filled with what looked like fiber optics but turned out to be strands of crystal and provided a warm golden glow.

In his exploration, Aaron discovered another amazing feature. Hidden in the outer portion of the bathroom privacy wall was a button which, when pushed, caused an entire kitchenette to appear sans table and chairs.

A tiny sink, a food dispenser and plates with utensils.

The food dispenser was mystifying, producing a thick gross looking yellow paste that reminded him of his nephew's diapers but somehow smelled like food. He couldn't bring himself to touch the ugly mess.

Aaron wasn't as finicky and dipped the tip of his finger in, looking thoughtful as he tasted it. Reminiscent of macaroni and cheese. A little off but close.

He nodded. "I think we just need to dial in what we want. I'll look at it again in a bit."

He wandered off to the restroom and Jeff went to relax in the cocoon across the room.

He was feeling tired so chose a scene with trickling water, very soft music and a view of the skies from Titan.

Returning, Aaron quietly headed for bed himself, choosing a similar ambiance after turning the lights down with the little switch just at the back of the vase.

Sometime later, feeling a bit groggy still, Jeff rose, hearing a clamor from outside the dome. He watched as the guards returned and caught a glimpse of Sioned and Aelwen in the bubble.

They disembarked into the city airlock and quickly disappeared.

Aaron joined him, rubbing a hand over his hair. "What's up, bro?" He peered into the crowd and caught sight of the Fen-Folk being rounded up and put into the still empty maben dome.

A guard was set and the rest headed for the city to celebrate their success.

Having had a decently long rest, Aelwen was refreshed with a short visit to her quarters and asked that Jeff and Aaron be brought to the common room.

She didn't have any time left if she wished to retrieve their ship. She smiled and rose as they entered the room, ushering them to the table with a wave of her hand and sinking back into her chair.

The food on the table looked and smelled delicious and Aaron determined to pick someone's brain regarding the controls on their food dispenser at the earliest opportunity.

They had been starved for food and company long enough that they made themselves at home

and began the enjoyable process of eating everything they could get their hands on, except that slimy looking seaweed. They avoided even looking at that as much as possible.

It elicited a gag reflex when Jeff accidentally brushed his hand along the edge of the plate and the goo stuck to his hand.

Aelwen noticed and laughed then remembering her manners asked someone to bring a bowl and hand towel. The bowl contained a type of enzyme that, when wiped on with the towel, dissolved the goo and he was able to resume his meal.

She, too, had a liberally filled plate in front of her and with a stomach just as empty as theirs, she dug in and didn't stop until sated.

She sat back, feeling tired again for a bit. She stood and walked around as she sought to increase circulation and regain some energy.

When she came back, their plates were emptied and the table was being cleared. She smiled at the two girls and wished them a good night.

Giggling as they talked of meeting their friends, they left happily after dropping off the dishes in the kitchen area.

Aelwen sat back down, making eye contact with the two men. "We have a special problem." Waiting for that to sink in she continued, "We must retrieve your ship or blow it up. Your choice."

Well that got some attention! "What do you mean blow it up? We thought you sent it back", Jeff tried hard not to look at Aaron.

They had been counting on at least getting word to Earth of their whereabouts. If they blew it up there was no hope ever of being found in space.

But, he thought cannily, if they could retrieve it maybe he and Aaron could escape in it. Subverting his eyes, he offered, "What do you want us to do?"

Aelwen smiled tightly as she watched the despair and then new hope flash over his features. With an inner chuckle she spoke, "We need you to use our technology to recall your ship. You know your security codes and we know voice recognition is prevalent in your security systems." She paused, "Will you do that?"

"Of course, but what is in this for us?" He pressed. "After all, if you have the ship or blow it up, we get nothing but kidnapped forever."

She hadn't anticipated this response. It was bold for a captive. Aelwen eyed Jeff appreciatively.

"You are not in a position to negotiate!" She snapped.

Leaning back and surveying the downfallen looks, she took pity. "What exactly do you have in mind?"

Jeff eyed her suspiciously. Aaron just sat there uncertain how he felt. The chance of a lifetime versus going back to earth? Hmmm not much of a choice. He could spend a lifetime learning here and never get it all.

"Could I be educated by your scholars, engineers and Mekhyr?"

Jeff shrugged. He should have known Aaron would side with them. This was brain candy to him.

Looking at his friend in disgust he thought before speaking. They might only be granted one wish here. At least for now.

"Since we *are* stuck here and there is no way for us to do anything about it," he raised an eyebrow at her, "perhaps you could see fit to let us wander around the city? You could put a guard on us."

"I'll think about it." She spoke sharply. They needed to know that they could not have whatever they wanted here. They were not to be trusted. Cute as he was while lying, *he did lie.*

Glancing at the guards, she motioned for them to return them to their dome. It was the perfect jail for air breathers as it took donning air bubbles to come back and they were never left there but returned to the airlock each time by the guards.

She watched the progress on the maben dome for a while, catching sight of her mother now and then. Her mother was one of the most industrious beings she knew.

Shaking her head, she ruefully hoped she could even come near filling the hole she would leave one day.

It was time to check on the preparations for retrieving the spaceship. She knew they would agree *because she would agree*.

Shaking her head again, this time at herself, Aelwen rose to go visit Eljarren.

There wasn't much time left.

CHAPTER THIRTY-TWO

Mekhyr thought he was seeing double as he stared into the microscope. Rubbing his eyes for clarity he looked again.

Ever the scientist, he had introduced blood from each of the earthers to two of the vials.

The genome had cloned itself. This could be the result they had been hoping for. But was the dna altered enough to result in the ability to procreate?

That would be a whole other series of tests and he would need to reawaken his specimen. That would cause too much damage of the nervous system so it would have to wait, but what did he have but time?

Layers of secrets permeated his existence. Mekhyr also had lab created clones of beings able to procreate as humans did. These were to receive the genome packages when ready. For now, until he had them all, they remained in stasis.

The genome packages contained a key to open the subconscious mind of the new being, enough to move the essence of the fallen to the new bodies.

He reviewed the data one last time and decided to visit Titan.

Something nobody here knew was that Mekhyr needed no spacecraft to enter space nor to move around in Kyra.

It was such a well-kept secret that even Gwyndolyn knew nothing of it. The fallen still had all their angel powers except permanent immortality.

They flew, they needed no air to breathe, they moved around in space as easily as walking from one room to another, they could be invisible and do things deemed to be *magic* in the mortal realms.

They could create, but not as the One did. Theirs was scientific creation, understanding far, far more than man about the nature of science though they were able to manipulate matter and space through the power of belief. *With belief the size of a mustard seed.*

Their ability to relocate physically and instantaneously to other places was only one more aspect of their being.

The feeling of loss was still overwhelming and still pushed away. To feel such pain was to invite insanity. Every fallen one had spent eternity with the One God.

Until they decided to abandon Him. Until they were slapped for it and faced the fact they would eventually perish, it meant nothing. One *does* never know what one had until it is gone.

There was a flash and he was on Titan. He flew over the area they left behind, searching for anything that would lead to the caves that housed their cities.

The fewer signs left for new beings untried in space, the better for everyone. Earthers especially!

Their thirst for conquest had already caused considerable trouble.

Titan was one of his favorite places with the view of Saturn. The wonders of the heavens were full of the same surreal quality.

There was no doubt the One had outdone Himself with the realm of mortals. Beauty was endless.

Curious, there had been a shimmer just there. Mekhyr turned and soared lower. There it was again. He was pretty sure it was a remnant of the *magic* used by the fairies. It appeared to be hiding something.

Landing, Mekhyr strode to the shimmer. Even angels found it difficult to see past fairy magic. He felt around within it. His hand closed on something and he drew it out.

A makeshift time capsule. Something one of the children had created. He thought about opening it but felt as though he were breaking confidence.

He couldn't imagine anyone else even noticing, let alone recognizing the glamour. So, putting the time capsule back, Mekhyr spread his wings and leapt back into the sky, floating in the cross winds, twirling up and up until he was viewing Titan and Saturn, Dione and Jupiter, Enceladus and all the stars, moons and suns of the Universe as he withdrew deeper and deeper backwards into the next dimension.

He found the wormhole to hell and passed it by quickly. The fear all fallen had was of being pulled into that abominable place. For sure they deserved it, but they had not denied God.

They had simply gone behind His back so to speak and then discovered He had seen them anyway. As angels before the change, they had mated with women and other females wherever they chose.

They *had* procreated. The offspring were used as the original DNA base for those the fallen later created that got them in trouble. Those that led to Aaron when they had all believed the last of those were gone.

The dimension he stopped in was an air water mixture. Much as the heavens had been prior to the divide in the firmament. It felt like mist but more flowing.

It smelled like the scent of earth's oceans and tasted like dew. It was another of his favorites. It reminded him of existence before earth's galaxy.

He could float here through another eternity but he was not yet finished with his task.

Another flash and he was in his lab. That had been restful and rejuvenating. Looking at the date calendar on the wall, he realized a full 30 days had lapsed in his absence.

It was time to return to the domes.

Returning, Mekhyr went directly to his quarters on the big ship and resumed his experiments. He would see everyone next cycle. For now, he was content to just putter around the lab.

CHAPTER THIRTY-THREE

The spaceship landed near the domes early. Jeff and Aaron were still asleep.

She was on her way to Mekhyr's, excited to finally be able to examine it and the security system.

The control system was on standby. She was able to enter through the airlock without any trouble.

In fact, there were enough similarities between Mekhyr's ship and this one that she was easily able to identify each area.

Mekhyr spent much of her early childhood teaching her everything there was to know about his ship. It was a requirement of upcoming rulers in the event there must be a mass exodus to another planet or moon.

When she reached puberty, the lessons stopped. She was no longer welcome in the ship, without her Mother.

Only if he had to leave permanently before schedule would she need this information. He didn't foresee that occurring.

Aelwen stepped up to the console and flipped a switch. She had *persuaded* the boys to add her voice to the security programming.

"Lara, find video for, she paused, January no January 2." She finished with satisfaction. That was another thing she had persuaded them to give her.

She could have asked Mekhyr but he was nowhere to be found. Another one of his disappearing acts.

She was pretty smug about her successes in this endeavor.

The computer responded, "Aelwen, the video is ready to start. Are you ready?"

The voice was nice and modulated but seemed to have a bit of personality thrown in. "Sure. Let's see it." Aelwen settled into a chair to watch.

She sat on the edge of that chair as she watched Rianna fly out of the hole in the crust of Enceladus.

Equally astonishing was the sight of Mekhyr's craft ejecting just far enough to grab her around the waist with the exterior arm and retreating just as quickly.

The video showed the responses of the occupants of this ship and she realized abruptly that Jeff and Aaron had received such a shock that they weren't sure how to handle it.

When the video ended Aelwen took a deep breath and instructed Lara to erase it along with all backups.

Shutting the ship down, Aelwen thoughtfully headed over to Jeff and Aaron's dome.

They were gone. Probably in the city having dinner with their guards.

Gria confronted her as she exited the airlock, presumably having watched her as she crossed the clearing.

Hands on hips, she stood in midair, furious about something. Aelwen knew better than to laugh no matter how cute the fairy looked. Her fragile but enormous ego was much feared.

Fairies had magic and did not hesitate to use it on those who displeased them. They were also capricious and looked to be creative in ALL their spells!

She put a serious face on and asked, "Gria, what happened? What upset you?" Gria fluttered her wings furiously, "Jenna and Daria are flirting with Jeff!" She stamped her foot.

Aelwen always wondered how that gesture did not send her end over end through air like it would in space.

Mekhyr said it had something to do with gravity and that the fairies related to gravity in a special way.

"Why would you be upset by that, Gria?" Aelwen was genuinely surprised.

She had never seen any of the fairies be jealous but this smacked of that green giant. And over a big person at that.

She eyed Gria with curiosity. "Why would you be jealous," she corrected, "Especially of a full-size person?"

Gria exaggeratedly pouted and fluttered her wings again, tapping her foot now and began as if explaining to a child, "Size doesn't matter, Aelwen." She stressed her pronunciation of Aelwen.

"Fairies don't have to be little and big people don't have to be big!" She watched as the news of this made Aelwen step back and raise an eyebrow. "Explain, Gria."

Gria obliged. She grew until she was Aelwen's size then larger. Oddly she didn't stop at the ceiling of the dome but grew into the water while blowing bubbles.

Aelwen watched feeling a bit overwhelmed by this revelation. She felt a little twinge of discomfort and wasn't sure why.

Gria returned to normal size and said, "See?" Aelwen nodded. "Why have I never seen any of you do this in all this time?"

"Well why would I need to show you until now?" Gria tossed back haughtily. She spun in place and flew off arrogantly.

Aelwen chuckled but still felt that odd sensation when she thought of Gria with Jeff in a romantic setting. Shrugging it off she focused on the task at hand and went in search of the two men.

Just as Gria said, Jenna and Daria were shamelessly flirting with the men. She had that feeling again. She would have to visit the physician if this continued.

"Jenna, Daria!" she barked at them, "Don't you both have things to do?" "Go now and leave us in peace."

The two pouted much as Gria had but obeyed, glancing back at the men who responded satisfyingly as they backed out of the bubbles.

The Merwomen were nymphomaniacs Aelwen thought in disgust. Then she shook her head.

That had never bothered her before. Jenna and Daria were friends. She would have to apologize later, Aelwen sighed. Whatever was wrong with her?

Sitting, she faced the two who sat waiting for whatever was important enough to interrupt their harmless interaction with the beautiful mermaids.

"Everything alright?", Jeff questioned her.

"Yes. I just wanted to let you know we retrieved your spaceship. We can talk about it tomorrow." Aelwen rose. "Well see you later," she waved the guards over to send them back.

She was annoyed with Jeff and it wasn't over his simple appropriate question. It must be whatever was making her feel bad. It had her on edge. She headed for her own quarters. Time to take a break.

It had already been a very strange day. Tomorrow promised to be worse. The trial for the fenman would begin. She *really* hoped Mekhyr would be there.

CHAPTER THIRTY-FOUR

Jeff and Aaron were thrilled as they entered the water and spied their spaceship sitting near Mekhyr's ship, so close to their dome.

Jeff's blood pressure rose slightly as he fought to hold back any excitement over the fact. The guards were canny and would pick up on any undue interest in what he and Aaron thought of as their escape route.

He entered the dome as though nothing were amiss. Aaron, of course, kept his head as well but the second the door closed and they could see the guards heading back to the city, he whooped and pounded on his friend's back until Jeff winced and backed away. "We get to go home!"

This time it was Jeff hesitating at the thought of leaving. He wasn't sure why he felt like he needed to stay but there it was. "I think we should learn everything we can while we are here, don't you?"

Aaron looked over in surprise. "Thought you wanted to get home." He went over and flopped into his cocoon and watched his friend.

Jeff paced a bit and answered, "Well you know they are going to want answers at home, right?" He waited for affirmation. "We have to integrate to get those. Simple." He gestured toward the ship. "That can wait."

He grabbed a cup and filled it, carried it to his area and slid into his own cocoon with the cup close enough to take a sip.

He set it back down and took a deep breath, relaxing as he replayed the time with Jenna. Now that was the stuff really good dreams were made of. He grinned as he slid into sleep.

Aaron lay there for what seemed hours, reviewing in his mind all the events since the fateful moment they entered Kyra. The wonders they had seen, the engineering, the myths come to life, being kidnapped.

He thought about how they could sneak on board the ship and shut Aelwen out of the security system. Then they would be home free. He drifted off into a tryst with Daria. Odd how he could breathe in the water.

Jeff woke sometime later and after a shower and meal he waited for Aaron to join him. He had discovered two things built into his cocoon.

A 3 D version of TV with amazing information about life on other planets and a device that beamed words onto the inside of the cocoon. He could move them with his hand. This is where Aaron eventually found him.

The guards took them to Aelwen who happened to be presiding over the initial review of the fenman.

They sat through the questions and answers. The Muir-Gheilt had created a cage of sorts to put beneath the dome he was in.

He was anxious to be done and back in the dome they quartered him in. At least there he didn't feel like a sardine in the little crystal globes Fen-Folk maben played with.

Aelwen finally tired of calling him the murdering fenman and disdainfully asked him what he was called. "Kayrun, lady." He looked broken as he huddled in the little cage. His tail fins poked out the other end. Their tails were so strong that nobody dared give him room enough to have a full swing.

Aelwen had little pity for him and was sharply drilling him on what had happened.
Wanting him to show anything other than remorse and suffering. She could not accept that this had not happened on purpose even though she had watched the videos.

There must have been an angle not shown.

Try as she might she could not get a guilty admission from him other than that he had her and there was an accident.

He admitted that he caused the accident but not that he intended to harm her. This would prolong the entire case.

Aelwen sat back, tired again. This was such a painful procedure. "Take him away." She cautioned the guards to rechain him to the cage bottom for transport.

We will continue tomorrow. "Come." She called out to Jeff and Aaron. "I want to introduce you to your new rooms. They are taking Kayrun, the fenman to your dome."

Aaron registered disappointment, realizing they would be further from their ship and watched better. "But we just got used to our rooms. Do we really have to leave them?"

"Afraid so," Aelwen responded.

The men fell into step with her, rather excited as there was no escort. "Does this mean we are free to roam the city without a guard?" Jeff asked.

Aelwen, still upset by the hearing, instinctively ignored him initially but then realized she was less than diplomatic and finally answered, "Yes. Don't give me any reason to regret this! However you will have guides. They will arrive in a few hours."

Turning to a set of doors in the long hall, she waited for them to catch up.

Opening the doors, she ushered them in. There was some satisfaction in seeing their delighted faces as they explored the suite of rooms.

The amenities were far more elaborate and comfortable. The educational technology was showcased here as well.

When she realized she wasn't likely to obtain their attention anytime soon, she left, closing the doors after her.

Maybe her mother was in the city today. She left for the jump station to see if Eljarren knew anything.

Sometime later she left the station, mystified. He knew nothing. She had about run out of options, having checked earlier and finding nothing. She even sent some scouts out looking for her with no luck.

There was only one place left to look. She grabbed a bubble and headed for Mekhyr's ship. Letting herself in, she wandered about, nobody was in the lab so she headed deeper into the ship she had explored as a child.

She soon forgot about her search for her mother as she became enthralled by the rooms and their beautiful furnishings and artifacts from so many places.

Entering another room, she gasped and stumbled back. Gwyndolyn parted the wings surrounding her and her mouth dropped open as she faced the accusatory glare from her daughter.

She straightened to her full height and stared Aelwen down until she mumbled, "Sorry. I uhm I was looking for you everywhere. I didn't know Mekhyr had returned." Horrified at the encounter, Aelwen backed away and rapidly made her way back to the airlock.

Gwyndolyn sank into a chair. "Oh, what will we do now, Mekhyr? This was all so sudden, I am not sure what to tell her."

Mekhyr walked toward her and she waved him back. "Not now, please. I need to think." She left and quickly followed her daughter.

Catching up to her in the great hall, Gwyndolyn stopped her and whispered, "Aelwen, please. We need to talk and not here. Could you come to my rooms, please?" She had to tell her daughter what had happened and why.

Gwyndolyn led the way and offered Aelwen something to eat or drink which Aelwen declined. She didn't think her stomach would hold it down as upset as she was.

"What were you thinking, Mother?" Aelwen was perplexed now more than anything. What good could come of her mother and a dark angel?

They had all heard the stories of the Nephilim and their offspring. They had also all heard of the subsequent fall from grace.

What she had always been told sprang to mind. That the fallen ones were forbidden to mate with humans. But her mother was not human, was she?

Her mother watched her war with her own thoughts for a moment, trying to formulate an explanation for what her daughter had witnessed.

"I am not used to one disaster after another, let alone while Mekhyr was on one of his forays to nowhere." Little did she know how closely her words described the dimension he had been in.

"When he returned, I was in the city and was not notified. I came here hoping Mekhyr had returned so I could beg some assistance. "

She looked down a bit embarrassed as she attempted to explain further. Aelwen began to feel sorry for putting her mother in this spot.

She knew it had been difficult since her father had gone. Her mother had been convinced for several birth anniversaries that they could still retrieve her father and had nearly caused the complete collapse of Eljarren who tried desperately to give her back the love of her life.

"There has been desire on Mekhyr's part for some time now. I didn't see it. Rather, I suppose I just didn't want to." She looked back up into her daughter's eyes, hoping she would not see condemnation there. She was not disappointed.

"We must still keep this secret and do no more until everything is back in balance. Mekhyr would rather not wait, angels have little patience when they want something.

Taking a deep breath, feeling relieved by the care in Aelwen's eyes, she finished, "He understands I must be one hundred percent there for our citizens and must bring the Fen-Folk into a more civilized state of being. I also told him I would be there for him to convince when you take the role of ruler."

Aelwen was a little shaken by the thought that her mother would purposely hand the reins over to her.

"I will never speak of it." She offered quickly. She would never even think of it again! Not if she could help it. Triggering another thought, "I won't have to be in the crosshairs of loving glances, will

I?" She wasn't sure she could handle that. Maybe eventually.

"No, no meaningful glances my sweet girl." Her mother looked bemused and amused by her response. "Thank you. I am not even sure what I want yet and Mekhyr may still decide to leave for Parani one day."

After a good hug and talk about the issues they needed to deal with, Aelwen left for her quarters.

Gwyndolyn belatedly realized they had yet to discuss her daughter's retrieval of the ship she and Mekhyr had so dangerously sent away. Well, enough for today. They would talk tomorrow.

CHAPTER THIRTY-FIVE

She had had enough excitement to last a lifetime, but she still needed to follow through on Kayrun.

She made her way then through the throng of the hearings room. What Earthers called Court.

Kayrun was, once again, in his small bubble cage.

She thought unbidden of her mother and Mekhyr and thought, how much difference was there between wooing someone and taking the same with the best of intentions?

But this line of thought was not where she needed to be. Rather she needed to look at facts only. Emotions were a distraction.

This time Jeff and Aaron were nowhere in sight. She was relieved and disappointed. Another distraction. She closed her eyes and took deep even breaths to clear her aching head.

As the spaces filled with those related to Thara and those who were her friends, Aelwen brought the meeting to order.

"Brighid, would you please share with us, your knowledge of the Fen-Folk?" Brighid acquiesced. She spoke of the journey and near capture by the Fen-Folk, speaking of the captive Muir-Gheilt and Aelwen, then the way Sioned had encapsulated the throngs of Fen-Folk in a magic bubble that allowed free water flow and even allowed the fish access though once in, they could not get out even if not captured and eaten.

It was an ingenious act that saved them from the kind of death that had befallen their beloved Thara.

She caught the movement of Aelwen's hand and sped up her appraisal of the previous events.

"That's about as much as I remember." Was met with a couple good natured chuckles as the long winded Brighid shut off her microphone.

Aelwen smiled and asked next for Sioned. She could already see this would take several cycles to complete. She was losing interest by the minute and for that there was no understanding.

She wanted Kayrun to pay for the life he stole. Her feelings had to go on hold. Good, bad or indifferent. This was the most difficult part of ruling. Her mother had given her this task a couple birth anniversaries ago.

She heard Sioned as he illustrated the scene with the fengirl and fish, in 3 D. The way her jaw dislocated made Aelwen shudder but what really got to her was the equally disgusted look on Kayrun's face.

She couldn't help it. Looking pointedly at Kayrun, Aelwen queried, "That girl was from your pod, right?"

Kayrun nodded, "Her name is Hera and she is from a family group that are so primitive. We don't eat that way anymore. Haven't for so long even my

Da's Great Grandfather couldn't remember seeing it done. Her group originally came from a planet somewhere in the universe that they had never seen or heard about before."

Mekhyr had asked them to take care of the little pod long ago. He said they were the only survivors of a planet that went nuclear. "The dark ones had located their experiments on diverse worlds to ensure survival of their creations."

His voice lowered in extreme sadness, "I know this picture makes me look bad but I never meant Thara no harm. I wanted her to be my mate and couldn't explain too well so thought if she could just see how it could be, she would want to be with me. I would have done anything for her. She struggled to break away and I would have let her go but we were well into the dark waters. I was fearful she would get lost. I knew the way and would have guided her but she tried to take off before I could say. When I grabbed her, she swung her tail. Rather than get hit and possibly hurt enough to be of no use to her, I let go. She flew back and hit the instrument station Mekhyr keeps. It cut a gash in her side. I raced back here with her but", his voice lowered even more, thick with anguish, "she didn't make it."

Aelwen nodded, "Sioned, please play the vid of the accident." He started it and stepped back.

They could all see the truth in Kayrun's rendition of the accident. They could all also see the pain in his face and the love in his eyes.

The group whispered words of regret for their anger and judgmental inclinations. They almost all hung their heads in shame.

Aelwen looked around the room. They had already decided. This would be difficult.

"Let's take a break." She walked to the office behind her and sank into a chair feeling numb. This chamber was the only private place close by.

Gwyndolyn tapped on the door, opening it slowly. "Can I come in?" Aelwen nodded.

"Why do I feel so bad about not being able to punish someone for this?" Barely giving her mother time to enter. She had already made her mind up without realizing it.

Gwyndolyn put her arms around her, wishing with all her might that she could take the hurt away. "Oh, sweet girl. This is simply part of grief. This is perhaps not the best case for you to judge. I think I must take over from here."

At Aelwen's nod, Gwyndolyn left the small chamber and when Aelwen had finished crying and emerged, the room was empty but for her mother who sat patiently waiting for her.

When she raised an eyebrow, looking for answers, Gwyndolyn shrugged. "I let him go. What else could I do? He did not harm Thara on purpose but out of love he was guilty of removing her from her home. As punishment Kayrun will return here every twenty-first cycle of Enceladus around Saturn. He is required to help with the most menial of chores and to attend the educational classes for a seven-moon cycle."

She hugged her daughter again. "We need to develop communication with the Fen-Folk. We also need to bring them out of frozen time they are in. They are very capable and intelligent beings."

Aelwen nodded, "You made wise choices mother. Thank you. I am better now."

They headed for the common room arm in arm, talking quietly about the events since the earthers arrived.

Speaking of, there they were, having a meal and entertaining Daria and Jenna. Too late, Aelwen noticed Gria in the shadows. Her face portrayed an anger like none Aelwen had ever seen. "Gria!" At her shout of alarm, Jeff and Aaron looked up at her then followed her gaze just in time to see the ball of light.

Then everyone witnessed the most amazing thing. Jeff and Aaron began arguing over who was going to make Gria the happiest. The argument grew into a fist fight and Aelwen sighed. "Take them to their quarters." She told the guards at the next table. *Men!*

"Gria," she spoke in an admonishing tone, "What were you thinking? How long will that last?"

Gria laughed with satisfaction. "I might make it stay forever," she challenged spitefully. "He deserves it. He acted like I wasn't even here. All stuck on the Jenna fish." She tapped her foot angrily.

Aelwen choked back a laugh at her descriptive terms and at a feeling that gripped her heart like it would choke it. *Why?*

"Gria. Why don't you return to your quarters for a while?" She knew she could not make her but Gria understood hierarchy enough to acquiesce haughtily.

"I am hungry so will go home." She took her leave slowly. Flaunting her ability to do as she wished so the girl would know she could not be ordered about unless she chose to.

When she was out of sight, Aelwen broke into laughter. Her mother joined in her mirth and the two settled back for a humorous evening for the first time in at least one birthday anniversary.

This is how Mekhyr found them after worrying about the last time he had been in their presence. He grinned at the sight.

They were going to be just fine. He left without anyone noticing he had been there and decided it was time to visit Sioned. It was a visit long overdue. He was, after all, his dearest friend on this moon.

The two friends shared a meal and sat back to discuss the current affairs of Enceladus.

"Things change." You taught me that thousands of years ago. "Life is fluid. It comes and it goes for all except us but even our day will come." He cocked an eyebrow at Mekhyr. "Right?"

"Of course. I of all living beings, will be the first to reiterate that. I am just concerned because we will now have a larger area to stay in control of.

The mix will make it difficult enough but the geographical area, well that is going to be a challenge." He couldn't even tell Sioned the truth. Nobody else must ever know about the genome packages.

It would be very difficult to find them at exactly the moment of death now. If they were spread across Kyra.

However, he *was* excited by the possibility that at least the merfolk, both the regal Muir-Gheilt and their wild and wicked counterparts, the Fen-Folk, should be able to reproduce. The resulting DNA should be very hardy stock indeed.

He hummed a bit without realizing it, thrumming his fingertips against the arm of the chair.

Sioned knew his friend well enough to know not to interrupt him. Knowing, as well, that his *friend* was hiding the secret of a lifetime from him.

But then, all the dark ones did. There were some secrets not to ever be shared. He respected that, having some of his own.

Mekhyr let out a long breath, "Well, guess I ought to go do some strategic planning." He let himself out as Sioned pondered his words, wondering what he could possibly mean.

CHAPTER THIRTY-SIX

"Uhm," Aaron was finding it difficult to find the right words as he shook Jeff's shoulder, hoping he would waken really soon. "You need to see this bud."

Jeff groaned, "Don't you *ever* sleep?" He grimaced as he realized his mouth felt and tasted like a tuna made of alum. Gross! He sat up looking the direction Aaron was pointing.

"What is that?" The magical scene outside the city dome was mesmerizing. Gwyndolyn led the group of fairies and elves around and around the maben dome as they flung sparkles full of every color ever created at the dome.

They danced and intoned and the sparkles grew and melded and created a transparent shimmering cover for the dome.

Those who would tend the maben were all inside the dome as this was done.

When Jeff and Aaron arrived at the glass tunnel where a few early risers or all-nighters watched the show of color and light, they were told this was to protect the dome from intruders. Whoever was inside could go in and out freely. They could also carry the maben in and out but the maben could not go out alone. Likewise intruders not imprinted on the dome would not be able to enter.

For earthers this was a glimpse into the world of myth and make believe and trying to wrap their minds around this became more difficult as they watched. Jeff felt a bit dizzy trying.

He had to get closer. Could they get hold of a couple of those bubbles in the airlock? Would they be stopped and held or were they considered citizens enough to roam even in the water?

He nudged Aaron and inclined his head, moving toward the airlock to find out.

As they entered the water they felt the effects of the magic being used. Suddenly going end over end in opposite directions, eventually they came to rest on the ocean's bottom, disoriented but sound. It was safer watching from there!

A tingling feeling reached even that far as the unlikely band of magicians continued with their work. Jeff realized finally that this was the same feeling he had experienced by the maben beds.

The amazing colors of the maben ponds finally made sense. They were infused with elven and fairy magic.

It felt as though they had stepped through the looking glass into the world of Mr. Limpet. They watched until it was done.

Neither spoke on the way back to their quarters. Shock was a light description for what they were feeling. How was any of this possible?

Jeff stopped abruptly. That was it. "We are dead Aaron. There is no other explanation for any of this."

Aaron slowly turned and took Jeff's arm, pulling him along the corridor. They entered their rooms and sat, silent for what seemed an eternity before Aaron got up to make tea.

A feeling of depression had settled in. Aaron knew his friend was too shocked to think right now and he was feeling that they must be either dead as Jeff said or caught in some kind of warp in space that gave them delusions.

Either way was difficult to deal with and if this was real, well that was even harder.

He spent a good portion of his rest time watching over and worrying about his friend who had slipped into a state of despondency.

Finally, Aaron slipped out and went in search of anyone they knew. He happened to run into Mekhyr who was headed for the airlock. "Mekhyr, so glad to see you."

Mekhyr turned and smiled, "You too, Aaron. Where were you headed?" He looked curiously past him wondering where Jeff was.

"I uh, we went outside while the uhm, elves and fairies were doing whatever it was they were doing and Jeff kind of lost it on the way back. He thinks we are dead!"

Aaron wrestled with a way to explain what Jeff was going through and what he felt. Life had not equipped him to deal with anything of this magnitude.

Mekhyr nodded solemnly and tried not to grin at this revelation. Putting an arm around Aaron's shoulder he steered him back toward their quarters, "Let's go have a look."

They found Jeff exactly as Aaron had left him. Sitting there staring straight ahead, tea untouched and now cold.

Only now he was mumbling to himself. "Just a dream. That's all. Are we lifting off in the morning?"

Aaron looked at Mekhyr, "Can you help him?" Mekhyr nodded, "I've seen this before. Here, help me put him in the bed."

That turned out to be awkward as the bed kept swaying. Finally, they succeeded and Mekhyr left to gather supplies. "I'll be back in an hour or so."

When he did return, Mekhyr handed Aaron a parcel of herbs. "Here, could you get some hot water and add a pinch of these?"

He looked Jeff over, "This is magic sickness. How much of it were you guys exposed to and," he squinted at Aaron, "why were you not affected? Hmmm?"

Aaron didn't quite like the way the dark angel was looking at him but mumbled out, "Close enough for it to knock us about."

Mekhyr nodded. "But you, it knocked you about too? And you don't have any side effects?" Aaron shook his head, "Nope. I don't feel any different."

It made him uncomfortable knowing that he should also be feeling poorly but there was nothing.

Mekhyr took out a vial and clicked it into place in a tool of some kind. Then without warning he held it against Aaron's neck.

He felt a pinch and jerked back, "Hey, what are you up to?" He glared at Mekhyr who pulled a vial of blood from the tool. "Oh, well why didn't you just ask?" Aaron stomped to the other side of the room against his better judgement as that left Jeff alone with the creep.

Unfazed, Mekhyr proceeded to draw the blood through what appeared to be a filter of some kind and then into Jeff's arm. He was prepared to use another method but realized this was going to expedite the process considerably.

Jeff began to stir and Mekhyr lifted his head, "Here you go, small sips." As he held the tea to his mouth.

"What happened?" He groaned, holding tightly onto his head, which felt like it had been slammed with a sledgehammer.

Mekhyr frowned. "You should stay away from magic, even if Aaron goes there."

"Wait. What?" Aaron was confused. "Why is it ok for me but not Jeff?" Mekhyr shrugged, "You, sir, appear to have a bit of magic in your DNA. Any idea how it got there? Any family myths or stories to lend a clue?"

Aaron shook his head again, "No. Nothing I remember right now."

"Well, let me know if any come to mind, will you?" Mekhyr gathered his things, leaving only enough herb mixture to make a few more cups of tea.

He motioned at the small pile, "Better store this in something. Make a cup three times per cycle and he should be fine by tomorrow. We will talk more then."

After Mekhyr left the second time and Jeff had finished his tea and returned to rest in his bed, Aaron plopped into his own and this time fell into a deep sleep. It was about time.

Mekhyr walked, deep in pensive thought. There was only one bloodline among earthers that could withstand magic that powerful. The thought brought heretofore unavailable possibilities to mind. Apparently that one line had been genetically altered at some point by someone or some thing?

Though it might seem the fallen would know everything, they did not. One of those things they did not know was that a line of Nephilim still existed!

He had not felt excitement like this for eons! It was a line that still had power of its own or Aaron would have felt the effects of magic much as Jeff had.

The power of a Nephilim was special. Unfettered by any restrictions placed on mortals or angels, Nephilim had raw, unbridled powerful abilities.

As time went on, their descendants forgot how to use them or that they even had them to start with. Often because it invited shouts of "Witch. Witch!"

Regardless, he had a prodigy to train. His goal, ever the survival of his species, Mekhyr was sure Aaron held the key to speeding up the process without damaging the hosts of the genome packages.

Ultimately this would destroy Aaron but he needn't think of that now. He shook that uneasy feeling off. It would still take time. Maybe a few hundred annual cycles but it would happen far faster than if he had to continue the way he was.

Returning through his own airlock, Mekhyr hurried to his library. He was sure the procedure was there in one ancient tome but where had he buried it?

Never seeing any use in it as it concerned everything Nephilim and they were long gone! Well, until now.

About five cycles later, he finally emerged, still searching.

Maybe on one of the *other* starships. He left in the small craft. He would search each and every one until he located that darn book.

It was the only one of its kind in existence. He was sure it would have been saved by someone.

CHAPTER THIRTY-SEVEN

Aelwen formed a release team to escort Kayrun to the edge of their territory. Odd to think of it as that. The borders made her feel so constricted and insignificant. Knowing there were other rulers made her anxious.

It was difficult to imagine how they could have lived so long side by side and not interact! Seeing Sioned's bubble made her wonder how much the elves and fairies knew about that.

They equipped him with a couple torches and a guidance device, though as a merman, his sense of direction was impeccable. One torch was for his return trip. He would trade for two more each time.

When they reported back that he was safely away, she turned to other neglected tasks. First the spaceship of the earthers.

Entering the control room, she toured the various stations as well as the captain's seat. Looking for similarities, she recognized some of the features. Like the communications systems.

Taking a break, she sat at one of the stations that looked like it contained a navigational arrangement. Flipping a couple of switches, she located the on switch and then the monitor blazed to life with what resembled a quaint map of their portion of the solar system.

Very primitive. They must not have the technology capabilities the Enceladans enjoyed.

The map, however proved to be interesting, not for what it portrayed, but rather for what it did not. It was a glimpse into the lack of knowledge enjoyed by earthers.

It was no wonder they were on the *do not contact* list every other captain had memorized before training. To give them anything more than they had would open potential for immeasurable destruction.

She moved to the next station. Apparently, the engineer sat here. She pulled to scale images from the database this worked with. She knew it must control the entire ship.

Now to uncover enough data to understand what every aspect of this space boat meant. What she could do with it and how. Those were at the fifth station she researched.

Manuals, indeed the whole of a vast library in digital format. Primitive with that as well. It seemed that 3d technology was not as advanced as she had imagined with the infomercials she had watched on earther television.

Finally, she viewed the flat image of video from the day the earthers arrived. She was a fast study and after erasing the data, she left the systems locked with the master code she had managed to install.

"Done!" She crowed, to nobody. Returning to the city, she detoured to the maben dome. Unaware, she slammed into the force field. Shaken, but still able to continue, Rianna reached through and pulled her in.

"Well that was embarrassing!" Aelwen grinned ruefully at her friend. "How have you been, Rianna?" Rianna grinned back, way happier than Aelwen had ever seen her.

Suspiciously she tilted her head and looked at her again. "What secret do you hold, Rianna?" Aelwen demanded.

Rianna laughed, "Wouldn't you like to know!" She immediately disappeared into the throng that greeted Aelwen.

When everyone else had spent their time with her, Rianna pulled her aside and fessed up to her friend. "Will you swim with me, Aelwen?" This was a very special request and recognized that her friend would sacrifice much to do so.

For this meant the temporary transition to mermaid and subsequent surgery to retract the gills.

Typically, this would be done willingly for family. But Rianna had no other family young enough to be a friend.

The only time it was requested was for a wedding and only by the bride to be.

Aelwen considered the request long enough for it to be respectful then gripped her friend by both forearms and touched her forehead to her hands.

Looking up, Aelwen spoke softly, "Of course I will swim with you. I am honored." Rianna twirled with happiness.

She was happy for her friend.

She seemed to be the only female in Kyra that had no desire to marry. She was half-heartedly sure it was because she was defective in some way.

"When is the happy cycle, Rianna?" She stopped twirling, laughing. In ten cycles Gareth and I will make our mating public.

This was a ritual much like that of earth in centuries past when married couples were *bedded* by the wedding guests.

Only with the Muir-Gheilt, everyone swam in place forming a depth of about 15 rings facing outward around the happy couple as they experienced, together, the only time they would feel so free just to be together.

The *rings* signified the circle they remained within, bound only by each other while they made first contact at this level of relationship.

The newly mated couple would then retreat to the island to spend a few cycles together. There was no set date or time.

They would be in harmony when they returned and her friend would be unavailable for at least ten cycles before her husband's mystic pull on her faded enough to allow her to integrate friends and family again.

She knew Rianna would eventually take another mate, perhaps even a third. She felt strongly about the old ways and held to them regardless of peer pressure from the pod. But she would always cherish this first time and nothing could ever replace it.

Hugging her friend tightly, Aelwen said again how happy she was for her and that she must go to the city.

Rianna swung Aelwen in circles then let her go, holding fast to her hand as she stepped back through the barrier.

Aelwen needed to see how the rest of the cities fared over the last few cycles. She had been so preoccupied with emergencies that she had neglected other of her duties, which had grown since her last birthday. Her mother relinquished more and more each annual cycle.

She essentially acted as a travelling mayor according to earths way. She was also the one to determine if someone should attend the council for breakage of a law.

Of course, that was mostly for protocol as rarely did anyone purposely break the law, whether in Kyra or in the domes.

Aelwen stopped by to see the earthers just for reassurance that they were ok and didn't need to be watched like maben.

Aaron answered the door and motioned her in. "Hi Aelwen. How are you?"

She nodded and looking askance at what appeared to be an empty room, "Where is your partner?" Aaron led her to Jeff's bed. Sleeping like a baby after Mekhyr worked his voodoo on him with my blood!"

Aaron was still indignant about the way Mekhyr had used him and then hinted at something majestic only to walk away without explaining himself.

Aelwen stepped back, "Used your *blood*?" She studied his face carefully. "What do you mean?" Aaron said, "Well he stabbed me in the neck with something that took my blood, ran it through a machine of some kind and fed it back into Jeff here's arm.

Woke him right up. Said Jeff had magic poisoning or some such thing then told me Jeff could not go near magic but I was essentially ok apparently."

Aelwen blinked. What the heck could this be about. Maybe she needed to see Mekhyr again before going on her rounds. Those could take several cycles.

"Is Jeff ok now?" She would have to bluff her way through this one as he was saying things she knew nothing about.

"Aye. He seems well enough. He's been sleeping ever since." He shook his head, "Still wish I knew what the dark angel meant when he hinted there was something different about me."

He looked questioningly at her. She shook her head in response, "Sorry, only he would know but I intend to find out." She turned and left quickly.

Now she had another distraction. Would she *ever* get to leave this city?

Mekhyr had better be in, this time, without being wrapped around her mother!

That concern was alleviated upon catching sight of said mother in the middle of a gathering in the gathering place. Good. She headed for the airlock quickly before she could be pulled into the fray.

Entering his airlock, she glanced around and discovered a light flowing from the lab in the corridor. She never could startle him, though not for lack of trying.

She had always felt like the dark one could stand a little shake up.

"Hello, Aelwen, "He called before she ever even got to the lab doorway. He *always* knew!

"Mekhyr," she called back. Could he just read her thoughts too or should she actually say what was on her mind?

Well, he didn't answer that so maybe she was safe and her secrets were still her secrets. She had precious few of those.

"I just came from the earther's quarters and heard quite the story while there." She had been trying to pin Mekhyr to the truth about certain things all her life. She had no hopes of receiving that now.

"Do tell!" he responded.

"So, was it true? Is there something special about Aaron? If not, why did you use his blood to heal Jeff?" Surely, he could not find a way through these ironclad questions!

"Well, I needed blood and since he was also an earther.." he shrugged. He had located a weasel hole in her box! Would she *never* win this battle?

"So, nothing special? If not, why did you say that to him?"

Mekhyr frowned, "You question my honesty, Aelwen?" She shook her head, "No, just your motives, Mekhyr. Just your motives."

She sat and sprawled out waiting for the story she knew he would tell. Only he never started. Confused she looked hard at him and dared him to ignore that. "Nothing to tell, Aelwen. Just needed earther blood for a match."

She pursed her lips and muttered, "OK then." She stood, "See you later. Heading out to the other cities in a cycle or two." She left.

He would need to be careful or Aelwen would guess more than he wanted her to.

CHAPTER THIRTY-EIGHT

Mekhyr, Gwyndolyn and Aelwen finished their long overdue discussion regarding the earther ship and though nobody felt completely satisfied with the results, it was a decent compromise.

Aelwen would see to the removal of the ship's location signal and other detrimental features, Gwyndolyn would allow Aelwen to take over this situation and Mekhyr would stay out of it.

Understanding the danger and effort, especially on her mother's part, when attempting to return it to Earth, Aelwen apologized for not including her mother in the plan to regain the ship though hell would freeze over before she would apologize to Mekhyr as he should have known better than to send it back as it was and there was the little fact that he was nowhere to be found at the time!

The elder two conceded she was right, and they left the now uncomfortable meeting together to discuss other matters. Namely the Fen-Folk.

Aelwen headed for the closest airlock to return to the ship. She would spend most of the day there taking care of her part of that bargain.

Halfway there she was grateful to have a bubble on instead of a breather as she witnessed Jeff and Aaron's attempt to escape and burst out laughing at the shocked looks on their faces when their codes did not open the airlock.

They heard her and turned, guilt written on their faces now and she put on a stern scowl, pointing back the way she had come.

They trudged past her and when she was sure they had entered the city, she proceeded to the ship.

She didn't have much time. The latter part of her day was reserved for her friend's wedding. She was to play a rather big part in this as the closest friend of the bride. Her gills would be activated for the first time and she was a bit nervous.

**

Gareth was on recon looking for the perfect site for his love. She would expect a beautifully, well thought out, portion of the ocean floor for their special space, with a little privacy. For those stolen kisses and more. This space also meant a pre-arranged space uniquely their own in which to tryst and rest.

He was running behind. Still had to spin the walls. Magic is what held it to the shape. Infused with all the colors of gems from every planet and moon, for Muir-Gheilt magic was enhanced by those gems, they had discovered.

Having found the perfect place, he began spinning. Jeweled tones sprang from his fingertips and the structure began to take shape.

He made it extra-large so they would not feel confined. It should be easy to flow from one area to another and room to flex a tail fully. It should be like netting at the ceiling to restrain them when they chose to rest.

He would have to finish later. He was running late again, for a maintenance meeting of the guard. Since contact had been made and Kayrun sentenced, there really didn't seem to be a need for them but it didn't hurt to extend for a short while. Just following a gut instinct.

He never noticed the shifting of shadows at a distance as he set off for the city.

He rose in the center bubble and took a moment to listen to the state of their minds before joining in on the conversation.

It was some time before he returned to finish his work. As he swam closer he noticed a mound in the center of his new structure. Looking around, Gareth noticed nothing else amiss so swam even closer.

It was a pile of the most beautiful, brilliant gems he had ever seen, though some of the colors reminded him of the hair beads of the Fen-Folk and the gems laying on the floor of the ocean, lighting the living area. Those were the first-generation gems. Fen-Folk used them to bargain for items to enhance their lives as Kyra's societies were being developed.

These though, were different. They were of a quality that would make it difficult to part with.

He swept a few into his mesh food bag, ever hanging at his waist.

He just had time to finish the structure before returning to participate in his own wedding.

Raising a hand, he started then stopped as the gem he was still holding began to lose its color and the structure took shape without any real effort on his part!

He tried again, holding more of the gems in one hand, mentally spinning the energy out to the shapes required. When done, the gems were clear, depleted and empty like glass.

The new structured dome was complete, and he had not used one grain of sand!

Maybe there was time for a visit to Mekhyr. There must be a source for these valuable gifts. Even more importantly, there must be a way to know when the Fen-Folk were around. It was unnerving to know they could be surrounded and never even know it. These had to have come from them.

But first, as a special gift to his bride to be, he planted several of the most brilliant gems in the ceiling net, infusing them with glowing energy to represent the stars they never saw.

Gathering up the rest of the pile, he headed back with the bulging net.

The small group of Fen-Folk watched as Gareth left. It was time to return and give their report. Malik was not a patient fin.

He had an idea and if all went well, he would succeed in bringing their kind out of the dark.

Though not patient, he was also not as barbaric as most, foreseeing a more civilized future. Most Fen-Folk encampments had no structured life, wild and fiercely independent individuals occupied them. Nobody answered to nobody. It was tedious living and mind deadening to the point they might as well have been just fish swimming in the oceans of earth.

In fact, there were even stories of them eating each other in the not too distant past. Meyrick, the leader of the group shuddered. He had seen the girl, Hera, eat and could easily imagine the stories were true.

The trip back took a couple of cycles and then another cycle to explain everything they had seen and when it came to what they had seen Gareth doing and leaving the gems for him, Malik became animated.

The dreams he had of his kind having the same opportunities as the Muir-Gheilt might come true after all. If they could do it with gems instead of war, so much the better.

Digging the gems out would promote unity of sorts among the Fen-Folk.
The kind of unity they had never known outside his small pod.

***

Everyone, air and water breathers alike, joined in the festivities.

Gareth had his meeting with Mekhyr as the preliminaries were being directed by Aelwen. The after feast, the sea fronds and flowers, the lit path to the wedding place and the lit path to the new home he had built.

Mekhyr looked thoughtfully at the gems, recognizing immediately the power within them and wondering how the Fen-Folk had managed to locate gems super infused with power from the "package" deposited into the core.

Wondering even more how many such gems there were! Could they be mined without affecting the life force in Kyra.

He would have to investigate this later. After the wedding and subsequent feasting days were observed.

Being the one to officiate for the pair, he needed fresh robes so went to change as Gareth left to do the same.

They would meet within the hour with Rianna.

A little about the author:

True to my Irish and Scottish bloodlines, when my sisters and I were young, I developed my love for storytelling. Making stories up to while away our time. One of these was about a ship that headed into outer space and "The Ship Hit The Moon", accentuated by the loud sliding clap of my hands. This elicited uncontrollable laughter for which we got in trouble but we still found it funny!

Our adopted, *well we wanted her to be anyway*, Aunt Bonnie and Uncle Vernon, bestowed grace, love, compassion and determination upon our little souls and always encouraged creativity.

Feeling blessed to be able to, I finally find myself in a position to devote enough time to complete some of these stories.

I hope you find them as alive and exciting as I do.

J. Kay Shively